THE LETTER MAGE

THE SECRET OF
THE GLOTTAL MOON

By Alexandra Penn

www.thelettermage.com
@AlexPenname
edition 1: 04/30/2017

For my amazing support system:
my parents, my family, my girlfriend, my friends...
and everyone else who regularly puts up with me.

THANK YOU TO THE FOLLOWING PATRONS:

Schuyler "Shin Kerron" Howe
@ShinKerron (#DinD)
www.youtube.com/user/SKerron

Paige Reitz
paigereitzsocialworker.com

Laurie Penland

Betsy Casey

Teresa Heitman

Erin Casey
@ErinCasey09

Roger & Judy Novak

Erica & David Claybaugh

Dane Penland

JJ Melchert

Deb & Les Halpern

Renée Buchanan

Kate Airey

Table of Contents

These are the rules of
magic.

1. Once a person chooses their sigil alphabet,
they cannot choose another path.

2. You are not an adult until you finalize
your sigil alphabet.

3. The sigil alphabet is personal.
No one can use yours but you.

THE SECRET OF
THE GLOTTAL MOON

-1-

I didn't set out to be a supervillain.

Supervillains don't, generally. Every bad person in the world is the hero of his own story.

Except for this story. Alexander Normal is the hero of *this* story. The *actual* hero, not a delusional idiot like myself. He tells me all the time that I'm wrong, that there's no such thing as good and bad, but he's biased. He's a protagonist, which means he's a good guy, which means he's programmed to see the best in *everyone*.

Alexander Normal is an optimistic jerk.

I love him anyway.

But I'm digressing.

I didn't set out to be a super-villain. Seriously. The day the Fourier Monks attacked, I was freaking out about test results. I was going to study, grow up, teach, maybe have a family, and die a peaceful death on my little moon above the Land Below.

Of course, that didn't happen.

***

The day the Fourier Monks attacked, I was fourteen years old and in a poorly-controlled panic. The attack actually had nothing to do with my mood—I'm starting the story before it even happened—and anyway that was far from the first raid I'd handled. No, I was panicked because of school. We'd gotten a set of life-changing test results back: something we'd been studying for since the start of term, something that would define the course of the rest of our lives.

It was a career assessment.

I'd failed.

It wasn't even a pass/fail test.

Our preparation had been focused on introspection, on learning how to figure out our priorities, on being honest with ourselves. The test was supposed to judge the stuff we were good at: in a year we'd be required to submit our focus of study for approval by the High Linguist, after which we'd start meditative study to write our alphabets. Except if you asked the test, I wasn't good at anything. Or I was good at everything. One of the two. I scored even across the board.

Professor Discourse, my teacher, had taken me aside and asked me if I'd actually answered honestly. And then explained that she'd never seen test results like these before in all her twenty years of teaching. She gave me a note to take home to my moms.

My moms. Pala, the artsy one, isn't too scary about *most* stuff, but Esp is terrifying. And strong. And, especially before the events of this tale, she was an absolute enigma. Sometimes I swear she can read my mind.

I think Esp is my *biological* mom: I don't know who the man involved was, and I don't really care. We have the same cool, black skin, the same broad nose, the same dark eyes. At fourteen, we didn't share a whole lot else, but I've sort of grown into her shape. I got broader, and physically a lot stronger, but at fourteen I was still kind of shrimpy.

That was okay. My parents never, ever made me feel weak. Don't get me wrong, they were still terrifying: at fourteen I was learning how not to be a timid kid. Esp was aggressively quiet. She knew I'd fill the silence when I had something to hide. But they built up my strength. They never tore me down.

So that's what I was avoiding, the day the Fourier Monks attacked. My best friend Semantic Wilde (Annie—always call her Annie) and I were taking the long way home, winding through the iron-brick alleyways and silver-vined, overgrown paths. We were walking home down the hill from the Low College, just like we were supposed to, but we were taking our time. I needed to vent my worries. Annie didn't want to go home to a pair of overly-controlling parents.   We had good reasons.

She was walking on a ruined iron-brick wall, barefoot and risking sunburn, dress loose around her ankles and hair tied in a long red braid. I don't remember what she was saying: her mouth was open, she was perfectly balanced on the ball of one foot, and the sky was blue.

There was a loud hum, a crash, and the iron bricks around me exploded into chunks of rock. The seeds of vines scattered around us, something crumbled below us as iron turned to hematite—Annie fell out of sight. I heard her scream.

My first impulse was not to heroically rescue my best friend. It was to scramble madly in the opposite direction.

A dark shape hummed overhead. I looked up to see a blue, spinning oval skim through the sky—a sinocycle, their vehicle of choice. Heart pounding, I pressed myself to the walls that remained standing and stayed still. Maybe they wouldn't see me. Maybe.

One heartbeat.

Two.

It made another pass over me, but faded quickly. For a third heartbeat I thought maybe it had left me alone—I darted back to the hole it had pierced in the ruins of the sidewalk. "Annie?"

Hummmm.

I froze as the sinocycle dropped from the sky and hovered, right in front of me. Blue. Sleek. Opaque as a rock from the outside, but the driver never seemed to have visibility issues. A little disc on the front detached from the body and began to spin and glow, powering up—

That was the weapon, their gun—

I stared down the end of my life.

Then—out of nowhere—the sinocycle cracked and split in two. The carriage crashed and crackled—the man inside let out an audible yelp of surprise. Before it could shoot, the glowing disc rang a high-pitched peal and shot into the air, propelled by its own centrifugal force. I watched it fling into the distance and felt a shiver ripple down my back.

A pair of sensible, thick boots hit what remained of the iron road. Esp's long jacket flared out behind her as she readied her paper sword. It was a blade I knew well: made of wheat-pulp paper and careful folds, it had hung on the mantle at home as long as I could remember. I'd watched when she'd activated the blade, when the oil-ink sigils had burned hot and bright and stiffened the single sheet of paper into a rigid blade, harder than steel. I could probably draw the charred sigils written along the blade from memory.

But I'd never seen it used before.

Usually when one of the other colleges raided our village,

we hid in a basement and waited for it to be over. I didn't think we raided other moons. We were the nice ones. We just wanted to study, we didn't want to hurt anyone.

I was fourteen, okay? I was naive.

"You okay, kid?" Esp asked. She didn't turn to face me, and she didn't put away her sword. There was clanging in the carriage as the man inside tried to get out.

"Annie was with me—" I pointed, expecting her to go rescue my friend. Instead, Esp strode toward the carriage.

"Go get her, then," she said. My face burned. Of course. My mother didn't have to rescue *everyone*. I bolted for the crack in the ground.

***

The weapons of the Fourier Monks didn't use projectiles, like normal people. Or rather—projectiles are ammunition that disrupt space, and the projectiles of the Fourier Monks disrupted time. So the crack in the ground wasn't really a crack so much as whatever happened when the bricks reverted to pre-brick form, and the ground beneath the road went through a hundred years of erosion in half a second.

It looked more like a landslide than a bomb site.

Annie was unconscious at the bottom of the hill. The hill was made of loose rock and sand and dirt, so it was kind of hard to get to her. I slid down a little ways, heart still pounding a drum line on my ribcage. Being unconscious is *bad* for you. I'd read books where the author treats unconsciousness as a tool for getting annoying characters out of the way for short periods of time. That was stupid. You didn't get knocked out without consequences.

Annie was bleeding pretty badly from a gash on her head, too. Something hard had hit her somewhere important. Esp had taught me from a young age to *never* move someone with a head injury, which was distressing because I had to move Annie.

"Mom," I called up the hill. "She's unconscious, I think she hurt her head!"

"Hang on a second!" I heard a metallic clang and the unmistakable sound of fist hitting face. There was a brief scuffle and a cloud of dust, and then Esp slid down the hill. "All right—good job not moving her. Let me see."

Esp pulled a small book out of her pocket and tore out a page. The page she tore into three even strips, small and delicate and very much made of paper. Swiftly, without even thinking, she whipped out a pen and wrote strange, wet symbols on the strips in harsh black ink: her sigils. Shapes I knew well, letters I could even probably *read* if I wanted, but they had a deeper meaning for Esp than anyone else in the world.

Like everyone—like I would, one day—Esp had made her sigil alphabet upon graduating the High College. The process was long and intense and unique to each person: the creation not only of your own writing system, but your own *magic* system, your own way of interpreting the world. Pala had chosen to focus on fire and art.

Esp had chosen paper.

The first strip she laid on Annie's throat, and released the magic by smearing the ink with her thumb. The magic of the sigils melted into the fibers; the paper stiffened and twisted around her throat, stabilizing her neck. The second she laid across Annie's stomach, and it did the same to her lower body. She was safe and still in case something had hurt her spine. The third she laid on the ground, and it stiffened and stretched into a small, rigid sled.

Esp knelt and carefully moved her onto the sled. "Aleph, it's a straight shot to the hospital from here. I need you to slide her *slowly* to the bottom of the hill, then run and get Dr. Kenning. Stable's more important than speed. Think you can do that?"

I could. I did.

***

Dr. Kenning's office was crowded. I could see the line out the door from here. Usually after an attack it wasn't *this* bad, but even as I slid down the hill with Annie I could see other sinocycles doing strafing runs on my village. This was really weird.

Usually they had something in mind. They'd attack just the College, or aim at someone's house, or steal a resource they needed and we refused to trade. We lost a lot of iron and silverwheat that way. But this was just... random. They were looking for something.

Annie came to a little when we got down the hill. "Aleph?"

"Careful, don't move. You got knocked out."

"Okay." She stared up at the sky, still a little out of it. "Why did they come after you?"

I was scared, and refused to think about the ship that had tried to kill me. "They didn't. We were just really unlucky. Stay still, Annie, this could be bad."

"Okay. Am I gonna die?"

"No."

My eyes were glued to the downhill slope, so I nearly missed it when all the ships hovering above University Village froze. They stopped suddenly. On a dime. I froze too, ignoring the chill down my spine.

They weren't looking for me.

Right?

It seemed like they weren't looking for *anything* anymore, because in one fluid movement they all turned toward space and took off. They vanished into the light of the suns and the sky, and were gone. We were safe for now. Sort of. I didn't think the man in the ship that tried to kill me had gotten away. I didn't think it could fly anymore, not without the carriage for the pilot.

We scootched carefully down the rest of the hill. I left Annie outside the red-painted building and pushed through the crowd inside.

The hospital was beautiful. Someone, when they'd decided to build this place, had decided to make it a work of art. The foyer was small (there were only like, six healers in the whole village, and Dr. Kenning was the only one who was there reliably and not doing research instead), but it was centered around a small fountain of clear water under an arched, painted ceiling.

The mural told our foundation story. First panel: the Land Below, the planet around which our little moon orbited. In the mural it was at war, which was shown by a number of mushroom clouds imposed over the continents. The second panel showed the signing of the Ageless Contract of Peace, which was an agreement to create the utopia below. The third showed that peace: doves and hearts and general sweet imagery. And the fourth...

There were only seven people boarding the shuttle in the fourth mural, but in real history there were a couple hundred, and several shuttles. The mural only showed the founders of each College: six plus the founder of the College of the Gear, which had broken off later.

The Old University had fled stagnation under decades of

red tape and bureaucracy: a world so caught up in its own selfishness that it had ceased to progress at all. They'd packed up their instruments and their families and escaped to the sky, where there was no Ageless Contract, where there was freedom. Freedom, but no peace.

There was peace on the Land Below, everyone said that. But at what cost? What was the point of having a culture if you didn't move forward? Privately, I questioned that: it barely took a week up in space for the refugees of the Old University to start fighting amongst themselves, splitting into the seven Colleges we had now. There had to be *some* sort of balance. Even now we lived in a constantly-shifting tide of condemnations and alliances.

We were not, I assumed, currently friends with the Fourier Monks.

Right now you could barely see the murals, there were so many people inside the hospital. There didn't seem to be anyone else that was seriously injured, but people were crowding around Dr. Kenning anyway—an older, milky-skinned, gray-bearded blood mage. Mostly they were asking questions: "How many casualties?" "Is the High Linguist okay?" "Did my dad come in here?"

My situation was a little more pressing.

"Dr. Kenning—Annie's hurt. Head injury. She's outside."

He pushed the crowd aside without a word. The man had failings—he was our only doctor, but he was nowhere near as good as the doctor we'd had before him. But he was decisive. He got things done. He followed me to Annie and I helped him carry the sled inside, through a miraculously-clear path in the crowd, and to a private room.

***

Annie lived down the street from me, but University Village was small: pretty much everyone lived down the street from me. She lived down the street from the hospital, too.

The Wilde house was a small, flat iron-brick building. It was mostly sparsely decorated and kind of ugly, which meant you could see Annie's bright pink window curtains from a few blocks away. To put it in Annie's words, her parents had never been big on decorating. The house was kind of bare.

I didn't like them much.

This had *nothing at all* to do with the fact that Annie's father was the Master of Letters, the ultimate disciplinarian of the Low College where we went to school. He was our teachers' supervisor, the author of our curriculum, and the only one with the authority to suspend or expel a student. Most people found him kind of intimidating: his office at the Low College was tall and big and full of a truly *enormous* number of clocks.

He didn't scare me. It was hard to be afraid of someone who got tossed around by his family as much as the Master of Letters was.

I knocked, he answered. A fat little gray man with a fat little gray mustache. Not that I was biased.

He also talked. A lot.

"Mr. Wilde-"

"That's Master of Letters to you, Aleph. Have you seen Annie?"

"She-"

"That girl is *always late,* Aleph. I don't know *why* she doesn't pick up on some of your ambition. You know, I tell her, I try and try to get her interested in her thesis, it's coming up far faster than you think at your age-"

"Sir-"

"But she refuses to listen to me. I wonder if your mother would-"

"*SIR ANNIE IS IN THE HOSPITAL.*"

For once he shut up, suddenly wordless. He grabbed his coat, pushed past me, and locked the door behind him.

"Go home, Aleph—let your mothers know you're all right. You can come see Annie tomorrow."

I didn't want to. I was worried about her. But he was right. Pala and Esp would want to know what was going on.

***

Home.

These days, Alexander and I share an honest-to-goodness castle, full of statues of us in heroic poses and libraries that could make a grown man weep. I have a four-poster bed made of gold and a bedroom with a view of the galaxy on clear nights. We have a *throne room.* But the house I grew up in will always be home.

Esp's great-grandfather built that house: it's been a keystone of University Village since the College of the Glottal Moon was founded. The whole building looks like it was made of paper: book-thin sheets of silver, etched with passages of my great-great-grandfather's favorite books, are plastered over the iron bricks that make up the walls of my house.

Obsidian windows from long-gone and distant volcanoes let in huge swaths of natural, muted light. Delicate, obsidian-glass chimneys lit the place at night, and from the window of my bedroom I could see Pala's fire garden, where she practiced her magic.

Home was where I did my homework among my mom's fire sculptures. Home was where I listened to my moms bicker (Esp never did the dishes! Pala always put too much garlic in the food!) and tease each other. Home was never low on love, even in the middle of the worst fights, and it was a safe place even when I was scared. Maybe it's part of being an adult, losing that security, but I've never had a place in the world that I loved so much.

Even now.

Home.

When I got there, Pala was working in the fire garden. This was a sight to behold on the best of days: my slight, pale, mousy mom dressed up in protective gear and goggles twice the size of her head. Her work involved lots of metal sticking out of the yard in odd angles, setting herself on fire in controlled circumstances, and scrawling her sigils on statues and plates with fatty, flammable pastel crayons. Her works-in-progress looked almost industrial, graffiti on unworked sheets of nickel and iron.

Or silver, in this case.

I came home just as she was finishing her final sigil. Pala stepped back and snapped her gloved fingers, which ignited a small mechanism that engulfed her hand in flame. Without hesitation she stepped forward and pressed her hand into the middle of the blue, rippling letters. They shot up in fire.

The sheet metal twisted and clicked, shrank, bent and reformed- and suddenly I was looking at a small, real-time replica of University Village, sitting atop a table of worked silver. The buildings were surprisingly accurate for flickering plasma; bits of metallic imperfections and interferences gave the flames different colors. This was a little more complicated than her usual artwork.

Most of the time, Pala was in the business of cascading, burning fountains. I didn't know she could do intricate work like this, too.

Esp was standing behind her. Pala was a wisp, but she was bright and stole the focus of a room; Esp, huge, had an odd talent for blending into the background. I didn't notice her until she spoke: "It looks beautiful."

Pala jumped. I guess she hadn't noticed Esp either. Neither of them had noticed *me* yet, and I was just standing in the doorway.

"I'm going to *kill* you," she said, and kissed her. My moms held each other tightly for a moment, and then Pala slapped Esp lightly on the cheek. It was more ceremonial than anything else. "You went to talk to him before you came to check on me?"

Him?

"He was on the way," said Esp. "We're meeting up tonight, I didn't linger." Her laugh was low and full of relief. "I'm sorry, Pala. Of course I was worried about you-"

"I was worried about *you two.* I saw it near where Aleph walks home-"

"He's fine, I got them before they got him."

There was a beat in the conversation as Pala digested that and Esp realized what she'd said.

"*Before they got him.*"

"I mean-"

"What do you mean *before they got him.*"

"Pala, it wasn't that bad-"

Intervention time. I made myself known. "One of them cornered me and Annie when we were walking home-"

Pala didn't skip a beat. "See? That's our son. Good kid. Doesn't lie. Doesn't try to make me feel better. Esp, tell me what happened right now."

"I'm supposed to-"

"You're supposed to *report in* and be all intense and important and help run the town or whatever it is they pay you to do. Yes. I know. It may come as a shock, but I know you pretty well. So before you go you are going to sit down and tell your wife exactly how our son was in danger. You are going to be honest. You are going to tell me the *whole story.* Are we clear?"

It sounded rough, but you needed the context. Esp had a fond smile on her face. Pala's arms were still around her waist, holding her tight, a little afraid to let go. Not everyone understood my moms: they had two powerful personalities, and when they argued they rarely pulled their proverbial punches. They had a secret to fighting that kept things civil, but you had to know them well to fully understand it.

Not that it was a complicated secret: they just loved each other, and they remembered it. Someone who loved you wasn't going to try and harm you personally, even when they disagreed. When they fought, they fought with opinions. Everyone got the benefit of the doubt.

This was something I forgot for a while, once upon a time. But it's a good rule. I regret that I didn't always follow it.

"We're clear," said Esp. "Aleph, go get your homework done. You already know what happened."

*****

My bedroom was blue-silver in the day, shifting to reddish-purple after the suns set. From my bed (big, but so full of blankets and pillows that Pala joked there was no room left for me) I was safe: Pala's art flickered comfortably outside, and my moms' bedroom was right down the hall should something bad happen. I could hear them when they went to bed, or hear them move around the house if they were up late.

Meaning I couldn't hear their conversation, but I heard when Esp left. I could hear Pala making dinner as I finished up my homework—a complicated orchestra of hissing, crackling flame—and I could hear Esp when she came back, just before they called me down to eat.

Homework was normal.

Dinner was normal.

After dinner was normal, but Esp wouldn't tell me anything about where she'd been. Pala had learned not to ask by now.

It was midnight by the time something weird happened. I was having a hard time sleeping: worries about Annie and myself and my village kept me up. So I was awake when I heard one of my moms leave their bedroom in the middle of the night.

Which never happened. When they were out, they were out. I took advantage of that and snuck out all the time.

Naturally, I followed.

***

Esp made a beeline for the High Linguist's tower. She wasn't sneaking, exactly: the cloak was clearly to defend against the cold (as my pajama-wearing self soon discovered) and she walked freely, not just in the shadows. *I* snuck, following at a distance, which made it difficult to keep up once she went inside. I was locked out at the door.

I waited in the shadows for a bit, looking for an opening. It didn't take long for Dr. Kenning to show up. And Professor Discourse. And even the Master of Letters, Annie's dad. These were important people. Including my mom. Who didn't have a fancy title like many of them did, which made it easy to forget sometimes that they listened to her.

There was no way I was going home and not hearing what they were up to. This had to be about the afternoon raid. I knew the inside of the tower: one circular room, and a spiraling staircase that hugged the walls up to the rooms of the High Linguist. No place to get in and nowhere to hide.

Not down here, anyway.

But the staircase was lined with windows, which opened to let in a breeze. And maybe inquiring young minds like mine.

I snuck around the back of the tower and sized up my challenge. My biggest problem wasn't the layout of the tower: it was my height. At fourteen I had yet to hit my growth spurt. I was short. Which is a problem when you're scaling walls. Fortunately, there were a lot of statue alcoves and artistic grooving. Unfortunately, the entire tower was made of sealed nickel, and that meant it was really smooth.

I hopped up to the first statue alcove and clambered up the front of a very dignified High Linguist Johnson (the man who last held the position, before Ingress took over), stood on his shoulders, and managed to swing up to the sill of the first high window. Keeping low, I peered through the smoky obsidian: the adults inside were sitting on tall chairs, in a circle, with the High Linguist in his nickel throne. I didn't recognize everyone, but I could see Esp, and the Master, and my teacher, and the doctor... The window was unlatched—I eased it open and snuck inside, keeping low on the stairs.

"All right," said High Linguist Ingress, "I think we're all here.

I'm calling the Council of Letters to order."

Council of Letters? What was that? Like the Master of Letters, or... something else? I'd never heard of a Council of Letters. We didn't have a Council of anything. It sounded like something you'd find on the Land Below.

"Esperint Worf, my friend," said Ingress, "you captured one of them today?"

I saw my mother nod. She didn't say anything, but then Esp was never really one for extra words.

"Did you learn anything new?"

"I did," said Esp. "He's still sitting in the Low Jail if anyone here wants to confirm it. But..." She paused. Took a deep breath. "I'm not sure what to make of what I learned."

The Low Jail was where you put drunk teenagers and people who couldn't pay back their debts. As opposed to the High Prison, which was reserved for murderers and treason. You'd think a raider would be in the second, not the first.

"What did you learn?" asked Dr. Kenning.

Esp was blunt. "They came here to steal away my kid."

My heart sunk. That was me. They came here for me. She was right: what in the *world* were you supposed to make of that? But at least—maybe—they hadn't intended to kill me. That wasn't a lot of comfort.

"Aleph?" asked Ingress. "Why? Did he give you a reason?"

"He didn't know what it was, or he's not telling me. He gave up his orders willingly, so I'm inclined to believe in his ignorance." Her face was hard. Protective. I remembered how strong she'd been, paper sword slicing through cold metal, and gratitude for my mom flooded my chest. "Ingress, this is my *kid*. What do they want him for? Why Aleph?"

Ingress didn't get a chance to answer. The Master of Letters spoke up. "It makes no sense. He's an average student, possibly of below-average ability. I can only imagine they want to get to his mother for some reason."

I didn't like him. Neither did Annie, and they were related. Esp was part of our little club, judging by the glare she fired his way.

"Resh, this is not the time to push your agenda," said Ingress. I couldn't see his face from where I was, but he spoke slowly and determinedly. "Copula, have you noticed anything about the boy that we've missed?"

Professor Discourse looked visibly uncomfortable. "Ah, yes. Esp, I haven't had time to talk to you about this yet, but he's currently our top candidate for the program."

Wait. What? What program? My mom looked pleased. She had her 'I knew it' expression on, a little smile with intense eyes, hidden behind the hand she was leaning her face on.

"Really," said Esp. "I'm shocked." She clearly wasn't.

"How?" asked the Master of Letters, appalled. "He's nothing special—"

"He's extremely special," said Discourse. "High Linguist, I mentioned the other day that a student scored flat across the board on the aptitude test. That was Aleph. He seemed fairly distressed by it, but I'm impressed. He's no genius, but he has a true passion for learning as a whole. That's rare. We'd be fools not to harness that love."

Esp looked proud. Really proud. I was suddenly embarrassed for not telling her—if I hadn't taken my time on the way home maybe Annie wouldn't have been hurt. And Esp wouldn't have been mad at all.

"They must know something we don't, then," said Ingress. "If we're already seeing the marks of potential, they must see greatness in him."

"Foolishness," said the Master of Letters. "They're expecting us to overreact. They're distracting us from something. There's nothing great about that odd little boy."

"That odd little boy is your daughter's best friend," said Esp, "My son. I whole-heartedly disagree, and would like it on the record that your daughter has better taste than you do."

"We'll observe this more," said Ingress. "And until then, Esp, I think your son is our choice for the student exchange program."

Exchange with *who*? The College of the Glottal Moon was all we had. Unless...

"We'll convene next week," said Ingress. "Attend to your families, make sure everyone feels safe. Resh, Dr. Kenning, is Semantic all right?"

"She's doing well," said the Master of Letters, "she just needs rest. Emily and I have been worried, but she should make a recovery. Thank you, High Linguist."

"Glad to hear it. All right. I'll see you all tomorrow. Get

some rest."

They began to disperse. I fled out the window before Ingress could turn towards the stairs.

***

I was too nervous to go to school the next day. There was a lot of stuff going through my head, and I couldn't meet Annie on our usual walk up the hill to school and talk it over—she was still in the hospital.

So instead, I walked until I could no longer see my house from the path, and then tore off in a different direction. The College was full of little twists and turns and ruins from decades of war, so I had a lot of places to hide. Toward one of the older, non-rebuilt quarters of the college, a small river trickled through the ruins of a building. There had probably been a real door somewhere at some point, but now the only way in was to hop along the rocks that protruded from the water, and duck through a sizeable-but-hidden crevice in the wall.

Annie and had I set up a little camp in there when we were seven or eight, and now it was our secret hideaway. We had a bunch of old drawings, plans for our alphabets (once we were old enough), and photographs taped into the ancient walls. Pillows and blankets, covered in grass and mud, made it feel homey and comfortable. We *called* it The Fort, but other than being hidden away it wasn't very defensible.

I slipped through the crevice, threw my bag onto the long, flat stone we'd dubbed "the mud room", and promptly flopped over on the floor. I took some time to stare at the long-crumbling ceiling. Crumbling like my *life.* Everything was *changing.*

Exchange student.

Esp hadn't talked to me about it yet. Pala had seemed pretty normal at breakfast, so I wasn't sure if she even *knew* about it. I wondered what that meant. If I'd be going to other Colleges. If my moms could come with me. They had to, right? No one would send me *alone.* It was too dangerous. I was only fourteen—which had felt like my first steps into adulthood before now. Now, faced with this huge perilous possibility, I felt like a child again.

Afraid.

Afraid and guilty. The test had been more important than I

thought it was. I should have just been honest and told them what Professor Discourse told me. Maybe then we wouldn't have all these secrets.

Someone knocked. I sat up fast. "Annie?"

"Nah," said Esp, and she squeezed through the crevice. She clearly didn't know what rocks to step on in the entrance, as she was wet around the ankles. But as far as I knew she hadn't even known this place existed, so you had to admire her tenacity. "So you skipped school, huh?"

"Not technically. School doesn't start for ten minutes." I gulped. "How did you know I was here?"

"I'm magic," said Esp, and she sat down next to me. "I read your mind."

"Your alphabet doesn't work like that," I said, but I wasn't too sure. I didn't actually know how her magic worked. No one did. When you came up with your alphabet, you didn't tell anyone what all the letters meant. Each person's writing system was unique.

I didn't think anyone could read minds, though. That was a new one.

"So why'd you skip class?" she asked me.

I shrugged. Esp's eyes were steady on mine, and she didn't say anything.

I could feel her staring into my soul.

I cracked. "I followed you last night."

"Really? I'm shocked."

"You don't look shocked."

"I never look shocked. Who do you think unlatched the window?" She cracked a smile. "Your mom knows you."

My cheeks reddened. I'd thought I was being clever. Esp was an absolute mystery, always one step ahead. Maybe she did read minds.

She let my nonresponse hang in the air for a moment before moving on. "So what questions do you have?"

I had a million. Too many to count. I had to think for a second. "What's the exchange program?"

"It's new," said Esp. "You'd be the first one to join." And then she didn't say anything else.

"That doesn't actually answer my question," I said. "What *is* it?"

Another brief silence. My mother gathered her words.

"We send you to go live with another family on another moon for a couple weeks. And someone comes to live with us. It's supposed to foster a sense of well-being among the colleges. It's a lot harder to fight with people you know something about, rather than trying to care about people you don't know at all."

"You trust them with that?"

"Of course I do," said Esp. "No one's gonna hurt a kid."

"They hurt Annie," I said.

"That they did." She was quiet for a minute. Took a deep breath, which was a habit of hers I knew well. It meant she needed to calm down and think about something—she usually did it when she was fighting with Pala, or when I exasperated her. But we weren't fighting right now.

"Listen," she said, "do you trust me?"

"Yeah," I said, "but if I'm gonna do this I have a right to know. You always told me I have a right to know about stuff that happens to me."

Esp laughed. "Okay. That's fair. I don't necessarily trust them to be kind, Aleph, but I trust them to be predictable. I don't think you'll be in physical danger. I don't think they'll steal you away forever. You might get stuck there for longer than anticipated, but that's why we bring someone of theirs over to our moon, too. It means we can be sure we'll get you back. And I think, if you're over there, you could learn a lot of useful stuff for us to know."

"You want me to be a spy."

"I do."

"I'm fourteen."

"You're also smart, Aleph. The school doesn't see it, but schools aren't always the best at judging intelligence. You're observant, you're good at inferring things from what you see. If you do this, you'll be able to help us solve a lot of problems. Think big-picture for a second: all the infighting, all the war—so much of that can be solved just by understanding each other, working *with* each other rather than against. What you see and what you learn will help us work towards that goal, Aleph."

It was my turn to take a deep breath and clear my thoughts. Esp waited patiently. Neither of us was uncomfortable with silence.

"What if I don't want to go?"

"Then someone else can save us." Esp patted the spot next

to her. I scootched over and tucked myself into her side, taking a moment to be a kid again. No one was around to see. She hugged me with one arm, protective. "I won't make you do it. I wouldn't let you, though, if I thought it meant I would lose you. We love you, kid, your mom and I."

I thought about their fight yesterday. Pala hated it when Esp kept secrets, and Esp kept secrets all the time. "Does Pala know yet?"

"Not yet, no."

"I'm not gonna have to tell her, am I?"

"Not if you promise me you'll go to school today. You don't have to be on time, just show up."

"Deal."

***

This time when the Council of Letters—whoever they were—met, I was invited. I walked alongside my mom and stood before the High Linguist, and I'm proud to say I didn't shake. Alexander says he's read about High Linguist Ingress, and doesn't believe me, but that's another problem entirely.

"Aleph Worf-Sapir," the High Linguist said, "your mother has told you what will be expected of you?"

That and more, I thought. She'd made it clear that I'd be reporting to her, not the High Linguist or anyone else on the Council. I didn't know if High Linguist Ingress knew that.

"Yes."

"You are aware that you may be away from home for many years, under this arrangement? That it may be difficult to contact your friends and family? That you may face danger or imprisonment from other colleges?"

"Yes."

He leaned forward, and for a moment he looked human. A little concerned, a little nervous. For a second all his authority, all his power, all his wisdom—it didn't mean anything. For the first time in my life I saw a figure of authority and didn't see someone untouchable. The exact opposite, in fact. For the first time in my life, the power was in my hands.

It was exhilarating.

"And you still want to do it?"

There was silence in the room. I could hear every breath, could hear my own heartbeat in the quiet. I met the High Linguist's eyes evenly. Later, I would be afraid. Later, I would worry.

Right here, right now, I was in control.

"Yes," I said. "I still want to do it."

THE BATTLE OF
THE FIRE GARDEN
-interlude-

When the first paper airplane struck the back of her head, Pala had leaned in to inspect a sigil. She didn't see where it came from: just jolted upright in surprise, momentarily distracted.

When the second airplane struck, Pala was annoyed. She *knew* it had to be Esp. Nobody else had magical paper airplanes. But Pala didn't turn around in time to catch her.

When the third airplane struck, Pala was quicker. Upper-story window. Pala caught a flash of her wife's grin before Esp hid.

When the fourth airplane attempted to strike, it was promptly immolated by rapid fire from a series of silver-wrought miniature biplanes.

Aleph returned from the Lower College several hours later. He arrived just in time to see one of Esp's squadrons heading off a pincer movement from Pala's Third Artillery Division. He stepped over the battlefield with a roll of his eyes.

And he used to get in trouble for snowball fights with Annie.

The Arrival Of
THE PRISM WITCH

The spaceship landed.

It was a relic. We hadn't made a lot of improvements over the original ships that had carried us to the moons: except for a tenuous, ever-changing trade that existed between colleges, no one ever left their school. We had no contact at all with the Land Below.

The Prism Witches had sent one of their cargo ships over to drop off the latest bout of trade goods—mechanical parts, mostly, and some pigments that would probably sit disused in storage for a while. Most of the color in University Village came from clothes, but we wore durable fabric and mostly fixed up what we tore. New clothes were a rare surprise.

They also brought their student, like she was some kind of afterthought.

The ship would stay here for a couple days while she settled in, and then take me back with it. I'd live there for a month, and go on to the next place.

My schedule: the Prismatic College first, followed by the College of the Helical Ladder, the School of the Gear, the College of Human Experience, the Unschool of Creation... and eventually the Fourier Monastery.

That was the plan: six months, six moons.

It didn't seem so long when you put it that way.

***

The spaceship landed in a cloud of silver dust and roaring noise. It was sleek and blue, mostly engines and storage space, and the whole village had come out to see it. I waited too, anticipatory. I'd never seen someone from another College before. Most of us hadn't. That was something reserved for our few traders and the High Linguist. And maybe Esp, but she didn't talk about that much.

This was new.

The door opened. A man stepped out first: youngish, but

older than me. Maybe nineteen. It was hard to tell, as he was covered head-to-toe: thick white furs, thick boots, thick purple fabric around his face. Obsidian-glass goggles hid his eyes. There was a spear-gun at his hip. I wondered for a moment if he was the person we were waiting for, but he stepped aside and crossed his arms. Ah. The trader.

Interesting, but not who everyone was waiting for.

It took a moment. I think she was gathering her thoughts, or maybe her courage. The light shone from behind her, the wind picked up for a moment, and Herschel Williams stepped out of the cargo ship.

She was small, and slight, and blonde. She had bright, electric-blue eyes, and a light, violet, wrap of a dress that was hidden beneath a thick, fluffy... something that she carried in her arms. Herschel looked around, hugged whatever it was she was holding, and walked down the ramp from the ship.

Esp stepped forward to greet her. "Herschel Williams? My name is Esperint Worf, and this is my wife, Pala Sapir. We're looking forward to having you in our home."

"Thank you for your hospitality," said Herschel quietly. She took a deep breath and faced me. "Are you Aleph Worf-Sapir, then?"

"Yeah," I said, and then realized that probably didn't reflect the gravity of the situation. I stood up straight and acted professional. "I am."

"I brought you a gift." She thrust the furry thing into my hands. "We are aware that your moon is warmer than ours, and my people worried that you may be cold. This coat is made of our very best pelts. I hope you cherish it as I cherish our new friendship."

She was better at this professional thing than I was. "I will. Um. Thank you." I looked helplessly at my moms. I was so, so unprepared. "I'm so sorry, Herschel, I didn't think of a gift for you."

Her expression said it all: *I thought not.* She looked up at my mothers. "Will the boy be leaving now, then?"

The boy?

I didn't like her.

Esp spoke up for me. "The boy's right here, Herschel, and I won't tolerate that kind of sexism in my home. He's leaving in a few days. Plenty of time for you two to get to know each other. Pala and I can grab your luggage. Aleph, show her how to get home. She'll be staying in our guest room."

***

I took Herschel back through the Palisade—a broken-down gate left over from a foot invasion, years ago—and into University Village. Herschel didn't say a word to me. She spent the walk looking around: the nickel buildings, the rusty roads, the bits and pieces of sigil magic that lined the streets. There were scraps of it everywhere, really. Stamps on the bricks, various art installations (including a few of Pala's), hanging gardens and sudden micro-climates as we passed by residential homes.

We were a village of just under three hundred people. There were a lot of us. I guess if you weren't used to it, there was a lot to take in.

But she could have tried to talk to me.

"So are you staying with my parents the whole trip?"

"Mmhm," Herschel said, eyes on a blazing rose that hovered over Okrand Street. Pala's work, from long before I was born.

"So am I staying with your parents?"

"We don't *have* parents," said Herschel. "So no."

"You don't have *parents*?"

She rolled her eyes. "Uh, no. We have standards."

I didn't know what to say to that. I had to physically stop my fists from clenching. I knew plenty of people who liked to feel superior, but most of them were older than me. Herschel was my age.

I decided to change the subject.

"So it's cold where you're from?"

Herschel gave me a look. A chill pierced the air. I decided maybe we didn't need to talk after all.

***

Annie was doing better. Well enough to list off her injuries, at any rate.

"I have a concussion, two pulled muscles in my neck, but no spinal damage! Two broken ribs, and a cracked collarbone." She smiled proudly from the hospital bed. "No surgery needed, just a bunch of braces and a couple brands from Dr. Kenning."

"Can I see?"

She pouted. "No. They're under the wraps. But he said they might leave a scar!"

"*Cool.*" I grinned. We were lucky—the only other College that could hold a candle to our medical care was probably the College of the Helical Ladder, the domain of the Gene Wizards. Dr. Kenning wasn't as good as his predecessor, but blood magic was pretty useful when it came to medicine. He could re-knit bones, stop bleeding, remove clots—all without breaking skin. Instead of cutting you up to get at your insides, he branded a sigil on your skin and let your body release it as it healed. Bones never repaired themselves at odd angles, infection rarely took hold to the point where he couldn't solve the problem...

As long as you got to him in time.

"So Dad told me something *very* strange this morning," Annie said. "Apparently we captured a Fourier Monk *and* a Prism Witch."

"We captured a monk," I said. "We didn't really capture the witch. She's more like, staying at my house."

"That's even weirder. What?"

"We're doing an exchange thing. Apparently all the Colleges agreed to it? So kids from different schools are gonna be rotating around. She's gonna be here a whole month."

"Why is she staying at your house?"

Awkward. "I guess I'll probably be staying at hers."

There was a pause. I hadn't told Annie about this yet. Since she'd been unconscious and everything. She rolled with it. "Is she cool?"

"Not at *all*, she's kind of a jerk."

"Oh great." Annie sighed. "Where is she now?"

"At home. I tried to talk to her, and I offered to show her around, but she just wanted to sit and look out the window."

"Well, at least you don't have to deal with her for a whole month," Annie said.

"Yeah," I said. "Sorry about that."

***

By dinner I'd learned that Herschel was perfectly happy to talk to anyone who wasn't me. She had a thousand questions for my moms, including but not limited to:

"Do you really grow your own food?"

"How in the world do you work safely with fire?"

"What exactly *is* letter magic?"

"Why are there so many boys here?"

"Did you two really *raise* him? Why?"

The last one raised an eyebrow from Pala, but Esp, unshakable, answered every question without comment.

"We do, yes, and most of your food as well."

"Pala designed her magic with built-in protections. It can still burn *you,* so don't touch the art."

"You'll learn a bit while you're here. Maybe Aleph can help you with the basics."

"They make up half the population, Herschel."

"That's a rude question to ask here, Herschel. Yes, we did, just like every other pair of parents on the Glottal Moon raised their own children."

Pala was playing with her food, clearly trying to give the impression that eating required *all* of her attention. I was getting tired of being treated like part of the furniture. "Hey," I said. "I have a question for Herschel."

Esp looked pleased for half a breath before the suspicion set in. I briefly considered that I might have had a bad idea, and ignored it.

"Why did you say you don't have parents? You must have come from somewhere, right?" Herschel rolled her eyes. Esp looked slightly relieved. And then I followed it up: "I mean, you must have a dad, right? Why do you hate guys so much?"

Silence.

"Well," said Pala, "You're diving in headfirst, aren't you?"

"It's not like you don't have a dad," Herschel said. "I *know* how biology works."

"Then don't make fun of my family!"

Herschel stood up, slammed her hands on the table. "*I didn't!*"

"You said we didn't have standards!"

"It's an objective fact! Your family units are completely unregulated!"

Pause. "*What?*"

"Herschel, sit down. Aleph, shut up." Esp didn't often raise her voice: she didn't raise it now. She didn't need to. "Now."

Herschel sat. I shut up.

"Herschel. Things are going to be different than you're used to, and you're going to have to adjust. It is *just fine* to ask questions, just think about how it'll be received before you say something. There's a difference between asking how our families work and insulting us because we're different than you."

Herschel looked at her plate. If I didn't know better I'd think she was holding back tears.

"*Aleph,* I expected better." And now so was I. "You're going to visit her home to learn about her people, *not* to defend our ways of life. Her people are raised collectively. They have biological parents, but they don't have families. If they're very lucky, one of the older witches will take them in as an apprentice."

"A Violet, in my case," said Herschel. She looked pretty proud for reasons I didn't have the context to understand. "Maiman Williams. I'm—I *was* her apprentice."

"Maiman Williams?" Esp looked surprised. "Really? You must be talented."

"I'm going to be the first Spectrum Master since Turing Lee," she bit back. "So don't take that tone. I can say what I *please*, thank you very much."

"You *were* her apprentice?" I asked. "Why'd you use the past tense?"

"*Aleph,*" said Esp.

This time, I shut myself up.

***

Herschel vanished the second she finished eating. I cleared the table, trying to keep myself calm, when Esp rescued me from dish duty.

We sat out in the fire garden, watching the suns set behind rooftops. Cain and Abel, our binary stars, were close enough you could only make them out individually when they got low in the sky. Cain was yellow and bright—Abel was small and red after years of feeding the larger star. There was a metaphor in there somewhere.

Esp didn't say anything for a second, just watched the sunset. I was too scared to break the silence.

I fully expected to be in trouble.

"Remember the lessons on words I used to give you?"

The subject was unexpected. It took me a minute to remember what she was talking about. When I'd first started school, Esp had taken time at the end of the day to teach me about conversation. It had started out innocuously enough—lots of talks about listening and phrasing your ideas so they made sense—but soon she'd started teaching me awareness of what *other* people were saying. At age eight, I was suddenly flooded with how much manipulation adults used on children.

It had caused a minor identity crisis. Esp had eventually sat me down and explained that manipulation is a normal (and often subconscious) part of conversation, and it's not necessarily malicious. The hardest trick in the world, she'd told me, was the ability to tell the difference between good manipulation and bad.

I'd slowly rebuilt my trust in grown-ups, but noticed that fewer and fewer of them trusted me.

"Yeah, " I said, "I remember."

"I want you to try and remember them when you talk with Herschel. In fact, I want you to keep those lessons in mind when you talk with *everyone* over the next six months. You're going to have a lot of people trying to manipulate you. This is important."

I didn't know what to say to that. I shrugged.

"Myself included," Esp admitted.

"I know," I said, and chuckled. "But I know I can trust you."

"I am your mother, after all."

"Also, you're the only one who warns me beforehand."

Esp laughed, surprised.

"So do you have advice for me on how to handle Herschel?" I asked.

"I do," said Esp. "Remember how I taught you to handle Annie's father? What technique does he use to manipulate students?"

"Break-and-Build," I recited. "He finds something to nitpick that doesn't really matter, offers his advice as the *only* possible way to fix it, and then gives you a task to redeem yourself. After he tears you down, you feel so upset with yourself that you automatically assume he knows what he's talking about, you listen to his advice without question, and you do what he asks to the best of your ability so he'll stop thinking poorly of you."

Esp hid a proud smile as she leaned forward on her hands.

"Good. How do you think I'm going to suggest you use that information in regards to Herschel?"

I had to take a moment there. "You *can't* be suggesting I use it. That's so creepy."

"I'm not. But I'm glad you recognize that."

Hm. Herschel was aggressive and loyal to a fault when it came to her home moon. But they'd brought her here on a cargo ship. Admittedly I was going back on the ship, but we didn't have any other options—while I'd never seen their occupants, I'd definitely seen diplomatic vessels from the Prismatic College before. They had other options, and they'd sent her with a bunch of spare parts.

"You think they use that on her. That she's not angry, she's just desperate to please them."

"Bingo. So what can you do to get through to her?"

I sighed. The answer was pretty obvious. "Show her a little kindness."

"You're a smart kid, Aleph."

"It still feels weird," I said.

Esp took a second to reply to that. "Words are a tool," she said after a while. "And a weapon. One I've tried to teach you to hone over the years. Like all weapons they can be used for bad things *and* for good ones, and what's the hardest thing in the world?"

"Telling the difference," I said. I knew that question by heart.

"Do you think I'm telling you to be kind to her because it's good for her or because it's good for you?"

"I think you think it's both."

"*Smart* kid. The best choices benefit everyone. I think she could use a friend. I think *you* could learn a lot from her before you go. And I think we—The Glottal University—could benefit from having a Prism Witch who likes us."

I thought about that. My conversations with Esp were always like this, punctuated by long pauses as we gathered our thoughts. I appreciated it. No one else gave me time to really contemplate. "That's not as bad as it sounded at first."

"I hope so," Esp said.

***

When we got back in, Esp halfheartedly chewed me out for being disrespectful ("But she's mean!" "Yes, but she didn't actually do anything wrong. You did.") and Pala praised me for standing up to her ("You're right, though, she was mean."). I went to bed that evening feeling thoroughly confused, and suspected that Esp had only been putting on a show for our guest. I didn't think she was really mad at me.

And then Herschel snuck out.

Well. She stormed out. She wasn't being quiet. She slammed the front door and took off north up the Okrand Tangle, toward the hospital and the hill to the College. I felt it was my sworn duty as a spy to follow her, no matter what Esp said. She was trouble.

She also didn't seem to know where she was going.

Herschel followed the path up to the ruins of the old College, remnants of some particularly devastating attacks on the early settlement. Annie and I liked to hang out there sometimes. The older adults remembered the ruins from when they'd been a city, and avoided the area—meaning it was a bit of a paradise for us local kids. We were technically forbidden due to the danger of rusting floors and falling towers, but no one ever paid attention to that.

The ruins were half-buried under half a century of overgrowth, but the paths were still walkable. Rusted roads wound across the hillside like weeping veins, leaching red into the earth around them. Fortifications and towers, half-gone from force and exposure, lurked in the wild growth. Abandoned homes were tucked behind them, forever hiding from long-ago raids.

Inside these buildings were scraps of life as it was fifty years ago: abandoned furniture and possessions, damaged beyond repair and left to rot into the earth. When the last battle had ended here, our parents and grandparents had carefully returned to salvage what they could, and left for good to build University Village around some established farmhouses down in the valley. What they couldn't salvage, they left behind. Annie and I spent long afternoons exploring the old houses, but we never found anything too interesting.

Herschel scrambled up the path as high as it would take her, then darted into a nearby partially-toppled tower.

I followed carefully, quietly, inching up the ancient stairs and watching for thin spots in the metal. This had been a watchpost once, but the inside was full of offices and crumbled furniture.

Herschel ran to the very top. I followed and hid behind an old, damaged bookshelf. By the time I got there she was sitting in the frame of a huge hole in the wall, legs over the edge, completely unafraid of the height or sharp edges of the metal. She was going to do something, right? Maybe she needed to send a prismatic message to her home moon, or was going to practice her arts in secret, or—

Wait. Was she *crying*?

Suddenly I felt awkward. She'd been up here to be alone, clearly. I couldn't blame someone for being homesick. I was feeling the stress myself, and I hadn't even left yet. Of course she needed some time away from us. I was intruding, not being a spy.

I stepped back, intending to leave, and promptly tripped over the half-charred remains of a nickel desk chair. I landed on the desk.

The crash was tremendous.

And I was tangled in the furniture.

By the time I stood up again Herschel was in front of me, rage in her eyes. She wiped the tears from her cheeks with an impossible furor. "What are you *doing* here?"

"I'm sorry!"

"Do you think this is *funny*?"

"No!"

"What did you *see*?"

"Nothing!" I scrambled back, but she was between me and the door. No way out. "I didn't mean to spy on you, I thought you were like, up to something—"

"Well, I wasn't! I needed to get away from you and your terrible family and this terrible dead-end rock, is that so bad?"

I'd tried. That was *it*. I stopped scrambling back and started pressing forward. "My family is *not* terrible!"

"Seriously? After you followed me, you still think we're supposed to like each other? You're deviant and prying and *terrible* and if you don't leave me alone-"

"We're not deviant! You're a sexist, abrasive-"

She hit me in the face.

I was *done*. Esp wasn't here to stop me. I lunged at Herschel and punched as hard as I could, just barely missing her cheek. She got me in the stomach, knocking away my breath— We spun— I got her leg and knocked her off-balance—

Herschel dragged me down with her and punched me *hard* in the face, again, blossoming stars behind my eyes. I tried to pull away, but ended up just dragging her across the floor. There was a scuffle for control, I got in a good hit—

And then I felt the wind in my hair.

Suddenly we were next to the crumbling wall, and the abyssal height stretched below us. This didn't seem to bother Herschel, but it bothered me. I did *not* want to get pushed off this thing. I'd used up all my arm strength fighting—even if I managed to grab a convenient branch on the way down there was no way I was gonna hold on.

Herschel used my hesitation to pull out of my grip. We both jumped to our feet, but she made it just a *little* before I did. The second I was upright she pushed me. I was looking her in the eyes —I could see her fury replaced with instant regret.

My balance reeled.

Somehow, instinctively, I reached out and grabbed the wall. I was just close enough to hold on, stumble, and fall *down* instead of out. I lost my grip on the wall but managed to grab the edge of the floor.

And hang there. My feet sought and found a hold on the nickel bricks beside them.

"Oh my god," I heard Herschel whisper. She leaned over and pulled me up. Her hands were clammy. "Oh my god, I'm so sorry—"

I channeled my mother. Deep breath. Calming down from the adrenaline. Esp probably would have done that *before* the fight, but... well, that hadn't happened. I wasn't perfect. "I'm okay. ... Please don't try to kill me again."

"I won't. I'm sorry." Herschel backed away and settled into a curl against the far wall. "I don't know what's wrong with me. I didn't mean to do that."

She'd been the one to hit me first, but I thought it best not to comment. "It's fine. I'm okay."

"You're bleeding."

I was. On my hands. But not badly—it could have been much worse. I'd grabbed a rough edge, but not a sharp one. I looked up at Herschel and saw a cut weeping on her cheek, too.

"So are you." Pause. "You should ask my moms for a tetanus shot if you don't have those at your college. This is mostly nickel but we've got a lot of iron and rust around here. Especially if you're gonna hit everyone who—yeah."

"Thanks," she said. It was a little muffled. Her face was buried in her knees.

I got away from the edge and sat near her. Not next to her. I didn't think she wanted me that close. "It's okay to be homesick."

"I'm not homesick."

"I'm gonna be." None of the other moons were in sight, but you could see the stars from here. They were brighter out in the ruins than in University Village. I focused on those. "I've never left home. We had an overnight party for school when I was a kid, you know? Everyone brought a bunch of blankets and camped out in the College. I was too scared to even do that. I stayed home. This is *really* new for me."

Herschel looked up. "So what did you do, then, if you love it here so much? Why are they kicking you out?"

"Do?" She waited. Something clicked. "This is a punishment for you?"

"Isn't it a punishment for you?" If I hadn't known better I'd have mistaken her tone for envy.

"No. They think I'm the best person for the job." I glanced over, even daring to meet her eyes for a second. "What did *you* do?"

She buried her face again.

I didn't press the matter. Like Esp had said, I had to show a little kindness. "You know, Annie and I hang out around here a lot. We have a spot we hide out in when we don't want to be around people."

Herschel peeked up at me.

"Want to see it?"

***

The Fort was dark at night, but still cozy. We had a couple candles stashed away for midnight jaunts away from home, which I lit. Herschel grabbed a blanket and wrapped it around herself, then blankly watched the patterns of the waterfall for a bit. I sat next to her and let her enjoy the quiet.

"I am homesick," she said after a little while.

"It's not like we're gonna be stuck away from home forever, though. I mean, you'll be back before you know it."

She shrugged. "Not for six months. If they even take me back when it's time."

"Whatever you did was pretty bad, huh?"

"Yeah. Williams got me off pretty easy, but I'm sure they're still talking about it. I don't know what's going to be waiting for me." She shivered. "I'd just earned my Cobalt robes. I might be frozen there for the rest of my life."

"Is that bad?"

"Yeah. Cobalt's good for someone so young, most people our age are only at Alani or *maybe* Jaune." She noticed my incomprehension. "We follow the light spectrum. You start out as a Red, then Alani—orange—and then Jaune—yellow—and then Verde—green—and I *just* got to Cobalt, which is only two levels below Williams. I'm going to be Indygo by the time I'm twenty, and Violet by thirty, and then I'm *going* to be a Spectrum Master like Founder Lee."

"Most people our age are only Ah- um-"

"Ah-la-nee," said Herschel. "Yes, they are. I'm good."

"I can tell."

"Most people *only* ever make it to Cobalt. Meaning they'd feel no guilt if they never promoted me again." She fell silent.

I nudged her. "They'd have to really hate you."

"They don't really, but... I'm a liability."

"What did you *do*?" She shot me a look again, but I followed up: "I can't be sympathetic unless I know, and you can't just keep dropping hints at some deep, dark past and not *tell* me. I won't tell anyone, Herschel. I swear."

"That's fair." Herschel took a deep breath. "Okay. This is what happened.

"Men aren't really cut out to be Prism Witches—don't give me that look, Aleph, it's relevant. Men aren't really cut out to be Prism Witches, so they're separated from us on their seventh birthday. For their own good, you know? They go to school in the domestic arts and take care of the foundations of the College while we focus on our studies.

"Technically we're supposed to be as separate as possible, but of course that's not practical. Realistically, you get to know a few who work in your rooms, your study halls, that kind of thing. Which means that sometimes love stories between men and women... happen. We're supposed to focus, but we don't always. Boys are distracting. Sometimes they don't cover up on a warm day, or flash you a smile when they shouldn't..."

Herschel paused for a moment. I couldn't decipher the look in her eyes. Half-frustration, half-loss.

"Everyone breaks the rules sometimes. I'm better than most people my age, but I wasn't an exception. There was this one boy. Lavinius. I'd known him as a child, so when he came in to clean or warm my fire, he'd talk to me. Not much—we didn't do anything inappropriate—but he was sweet. And I guess you can tell where this is going."

I could.

"My friends encouraged me to approach him. So I did. Put my heart out on the line." Her voice turned bitter. "He refused me."

"And they banished you for that?" That seemed like a small offense.

She shook her head. "No. They didn't."

"So what..."

"*Gods,* Aleph, what do you think happened. I was about to push you off a tower for checking to see if I was okay. What do you think happened to someone who *broke my heart*?"

Oh.

"Something's *wrong* with me! Men are supposed to be the illogical ones, the angry ones, ruled by their *other* head, and—and I'm supposed to be calm, and logical, and intelligent, and somehow —"

Oh.

"I don't know why I'm so screwed up." Herschel wiped her eyes. "They sent me out here after that. Master Williams said they needed to patch things up and decide what to do with me when I get back."

"I'm sorry," I said. I wasn't sure if I meant it. She hadn't really gone into details. She'd clearly done something bad. But I think Herschel needed to hear it anyway.

And I wasn't doing this to make enemies.

***

By the time we got home, the suns were already rising. We were covered in dirt and slightly damp. Herschel's hair had gone from silver-blonde to a muddy yellow; my nightclothes were caked in clay at places. Esp, thankfully, had not noticed we were gone.

Pala had.

She was waiting up with a pot of tea and a stern look, and we were stupid enough to come in the front door. We froze as soon as we saw her.

"Busy night?"

We nodded.

She frowned, concerned. "What in the *world* happened to your faces?"

Herschel's hand shot up to try and cover the bruise spreading across her chin. I wasn't even going to bother trying to hide the damage she'd done to me. She was dangerous, but that was nothing new. As long as she didn't fall in love with me I was probably fine.

Show a little kindness.

"Nothing," I said. "We're okay. We're friends."

Herschel glanced my way and hid a smile. Her back straightened a little and she seemed… better. Less angry. "I want to apologize for my behavior last night, Pala," she said. "It was out of line. I promise not to steal your son away for any more evenings, either. We didn't do anything inappropriate, I promise."

"Inappropriate?"

"You… you know." Herschel was suddenly visibly uncomfortable.

"We trust Aleph," said Pala. "You're not in trouble."

I knew her better than that. I was never in trouble, but somehow all my actions seemed to have consequences. "But?"

"But you've got school, Aleph, and Herschel, you have your first day of lessons. Go get ready for the day. And Aleph, the High Linguist wants to see you before classes. You're not getting a late note, so hurry up."

So after being out all night, we didn't get to rest. Pala wasn't going to let us skip classes in favor of sleep.

I guess that was fair.

***

The High Linguist's office was a lot less intimidating when I wasn't surrounded by a secret society. Ingress sat in a regular chair, not his throne. And he'd made me tea, which was welcome— I hadn't eaten when Pala offered me breakfast. I'd been too tired. Now the hunger was starting to show its edge.

I sat, instantly relaxed. "Thank you, sir."

"Thank *you*, Aleph. I wanted to check in on you before you left. Are you prepared for this?"

"Yeah. I think I am. Esp's been educating me on the major cultural differences, and getting to know Herschel before I leave is a big help." I sipped my tea. "Should I be doing anything else?"

"Have you packed?"

I had not. I had no idea what to bring. "Herschel brought me some warm clothes when she arrived."

"You might want to bring more than just those. Have you talked to Professor Discourse about how you'll continue your studies?"

Not really. I shrank.

"Decided what books to bring with you?"

Not at all. Maybe I wasn't ready.

"That's all right, Aleph. That's why I'm here. Talk to your teacher this afternoon, before you go home. And I'd like you to meet with me before school for the next few days to go over the cultural aspects. Esp knows a good deal, but not more than what's in the public record. I'll make sure you have an adequate education."

"Yes, sir." There was something off about that suggestion. A suspicion lingered in the back of my mind: Ingress hadn't needed to phrase it like that. He could have offered help without making me feel small first. And at the last minute? Why hadn't he offered when they'd accepted me into the exchange program?

"Have you been getting to know Herschel Williams?"

Everyone did it in normal conversation, to a certain degree. Esp had been clear on that, years and years ago. But this wasn't a normal conversation. He had his reasons for choosing me. I was pretty sure he had his reasons for putting me on the defensive, too.

What was the hardest thing in the world?

"Yeah, we hung out a lot last night."

"Are you comfortable telling me what you think of her?"

There it was: the task, the redemption. He'd made me seem

unprepared, but gave me the chance to prove him wrong—all I had to do was tell him what I knew about Herschel. I didn't know why he'd asked. It could have been completely innocent. But the structure of the conversation didn't *feel* innocent.

"Yeah. She's pretty nice. She seemed a little freaked out yesterday, but once she had dinner with us she calmed down a lot. It sounded like she didn't like her world much. Mom told me to be nice to her."

"Which mom?"

I shrugged and sipped my tea. I got the feeling that he already knew, and that for some reason it was condemning information. "I don't really remember. Why does it matter?"

"I'm just curious." The High Linguist smiled kindly. Before this conversation I'd always seen him as sort of above the daily politics that Esp and the Master of Letters got into, but now I was wondering if that was the case. "They're absolutely right, of course. I'm glad she likes it here."

"She does. That's the whole point, right? Fostering a sense of fraternity?"

"It is. I'm glad we have you on our side, Aleph."

"Me too," I said, and wasn't really sure what I meant by that. "Thanks for meeting with me, Sir. I'll see you tomorrow morning?"

"That's right. Bright and early."

"I'm looking forward to it, sir." I smiled the most innocent, oblivious smile I could conjure, and shook his hand before I left. I made my way up the path to the Low College until the High Linguist's tower was out of sight, and then decided I'd be late for school. Esp should know about this.

I took the long way home, careful and out of sight.

THE WITCH AND
THE WORDS
-interlude-

Herschel Williams had never been apologetic. It wasn't in her nature.

As a Red, she'd never felt sorry for the friends who couldn't keep up: she'd known from the start she was something special. As Alani, she'd never given the jealousy of her older sisters a second thought. As Jaune, she'd never let the young adults patronize her. As Verde, she'd never allowed the teachers to underestimate her.

And now, as Cobalt, she'd never been sorry about being the youngest woman in the room.

It wasn't easy. No matter what anyone says, people resent success: all her life, Herschel had been painted as stuck-up and conceited. She wasn't, really. She was just an excellent witch, and no one would ever make her feel bad about that. It wasn't something to be sorry for.

Tonight, though, she owed someone an apology.

Aleph was having a hard time packing: frustrated noises and the occasional *thud* of a fallen object had been filling the house since noon. She didn't think he'd mind a quick break when she knocked on his door.

"Hey." Aleph looked nervous. She could relate, but she wasn't going to tell him that.

"Hey," said Herschel. "Listen, uh, I'm sorry."

"What for?"

"For saying your family was unregulated. And implying they were strange. You've been nothing but kind to me, and I don't deserve that."

Aleph looked confused. And a little relieved. "Who doesn't deserve kindness?"

Me, Herschel thought. *I just told you.*

But she didn't say it.

These are the rules of
magic.

1. To manipulate The Light is to achieve true
connection with your sisters-in-brilliance. There
is no deeper love than this.

2. To access The Light is to be able to command
all the knowledge of our mothers,
to be able to store your own knowledge,
and to be able to transmit it.

3. Any person can access The Light.

THE TOWERS OF
ICE

-3-

It was time to leave home.

Esp told me once that everyone hits that nexus point at some part of their lives, but it doesn't usually happen so soon. When she left home, she said, it was because there was nothing in the world that could make her stay. She was older, and angrier, and pushed her home away with everything she had. I was young, and loved my family, but felt pulled toward a greater purpose. Totally different experiences, I'd told her, of the exact same life event.

She'd laughed.

That conversation happened years after this story, long after I looked back at University Village with my heart pounding in my chest. Long after I hiked my backpack up and strode out into the farmlands.

Long after I left.

There was a small crowd in the silverwheat fields to see me off, but nothing like the one that had been there for Herschel's arrival. I was all right with that. In fact, I would have been okay with it being a little smaller: I could have done without High Linguist Ingress' presence, and the Master of Letters clearly didn't want to be there.

It was kind of a chilly morning. I walked there in silence with my moms and sister student, already wearing the alien furs that Herschel had given me. White furs—the color of a guest or a child, she'd explained. I had been awarded no color on the spectrum, so I wasn't to wear pigmented furs. That suited me. We didn't have a whole lot of bold colors at home anyway. The neutral-blue cloth of the rest of the outfit was already a stretch.

Herschel herself was wearing an old dress Annie had lent her. I think we both felt a little inverted.

Ingress waved to me as we neared the cargo ship. The man from Herschel's arrival was standing silently at the gangplank, still wrapped in violet. I was nowhere near as extensively covered, but why was he wearing violet? Herschel had made it clear only women were Prism Witches.

"Aleph!" called Ingress, waving. He strode up to me and tugged me forward, away from my family. "I want to speak to you before you go."

"Um. Sure."

"Aleph," said Ingress, kneeling to face me eye-to-eye, like an equal. "This is going to be a dangerous mission. And you're very young. I want you to know how *brave* you are for accepting your call to arms. Our little satellite owes you a debt of gratitude."

"I'm the best one for the job, sir," I said, trying not to look too uncomfortable. "But thanks."

"You don't need to be so formal with me, Aleph." He smiled and hugged me before I realized what was happening. "It has been an honor getting to know you these past few weeks."

The crowd made some delighted noises. *Oh.* That's what was going on. He was trying to play father figure. I looked up at Esp for guidance, and she smiled and shrugged: *roll with it.*

I hugged him back and let the crowd have their sweet moment. But *just* for a moment. "Thank you, sir," I said. "Can I have a second with my moms before I leave? And Herschel?"

"Of course, Aleph." He ruffled my hair fondly. Someone took a picture.

***

I pulled them away from the crowd. There were still a few camera flashes, but at least we could pretend we had privacy, which was something. There was so much I wanted to say, but suddenly nothing was coming out. Words failed me.

"My friends are good people," said Herschel. "Tell the Cobalts you know me and you'll have a good group of friends. Tell them I've got your back."

Knowing her history that sounded vaguely threatening.

"Thanks," I said. "So you think I'll like it there?"

"Oh *Light* no," said Herschel. "You're gonna hate it. It's cold. But it's beautiful. You'll be okay."

"Thanks," I said again. I was never really sure how to respond to her. I also kind of wished she could come with me.

"You're going to be fine," said Pala. She swooped in and hugged me. I hugged her back. Tightly. Genuinely. She smelled a little like kerosene and felt a little greasy, but that was how Pala always felt. Kerosene smelled like home.

"I will be," I promised. "They aren't gonna hurt me. Herschel's nice enough, right?" I cracked a smile at Herschel. She laughed. She'd almost killed me a couple days ago, but my moms didn't need to know that. They'd worry.

"I know, kiddo." Pala wiped away a tear. "It's just gonna be a long visit. So. So we have presents."

"Presents?"

Esp smiled. "You go first, hon."

Pala had taken a large backpack with her, and from it she pulled out a small box. It didn't look special: cardboard, and with telltale stains that marked it as a handmade Pala gift. Inside was a little iron heart on a silver chain. It was slightly warm to the touch and laced with filigree designs, hanging on a chain of silver.

She took it out of the box and slipped the necklace over my head. "I know it's a little silly," she said, "but I thought some heat might come in handy on an ice moon. See here—"

Pala pressed a clasp on the side of the locket and it sprung open, spouting a little jet of flame from inside. She closed it and the flame vanished. It stayed warm against my breast, though, and I smiled at the comfort.

"It's perfect. Thank you."

"Stay warm over there, kiddo."

"I will."

"Show him the second gift," said Esp.

This turned out to be the backpack itself. It was full of books—which was a little confusing. I'd already packed my school supplies, and that case was already on the ship.

"Afternoon lessons," Esp explained. My moms had given me supplemental education for as long as I could remember: Esp in conversation, and Pala in critical thinking. Two things they claimed didn't get taught in school. "So you can stay caught up. Wouldn't call it a secret, they'll probably search your bags, but I wouldn't advertise these, okay? Oratory skills make people uncomfortable."

"Okay."

"And there's one more. This one's special." Esp pulled a book off the top of the pile. A small black journal, with my name written in silver on the cover. "This is a Bound Book. I've got a matching one at home."

"A matching one?"

"A *perfectly* matching one. Whatever happens to this book happens to mine, too. Anything you write in here shows up in the one I have at home, and vice versa. We can write letters this way that won't have to pass through anyone else's hands."

Now it was my turn to wipe my eyes.

"You're gonna do great, kid," Esp said. I tucked the journal into my furs, safe inside a convenient pocket, and then hugged her tightly. She was always Pala's polar opposite: she smelled clean and slightly of lavender.

It suddenly struck me how much I was going to miss them: six months wasn't long, but at the same time it was an eternity. My entire world up to this point had been the College and University Village.

My entire world had been my family.

"Thank you so much. I love you, moms."

"We love you too," said Pala.

Esp squeezed me tight, and then released me. "Go have an adventure, kid."

"Let me know how Master Williams is doing," Herschel added.

Pala fussed at my collar, one last time. "And don't forget to write home."

"I promise," I said. "To all three."

***

The Glottal Moon was a rocky, dusty place, made of hematite and nickel and dirt. When we weren't studying and researching, we were farming: silverwheat and tubers made up the backbone of most of what we ate. The color scheme could best be described as 'sepia'. At night, the other moons hung among the stars like dancers, drifting in and out of the sky as we grew closer and further away.

As we drifted into space, I looked back to watch the Glottal Moon shrink.

It looked small. And brown. And yet *huge*; it was easy to forget that University Village was nothing more than a speck on the side of our little satellite. My hometown vanished quickly. The Glottal Moon stayed. I'd be able to see it clearly from my place with the Prism Witches.

On the Prismatic Moon.

Which drifted closer, slowly. At this time of year it was barely visible from University Village, but even at its closest pass it was never larger than the nail of my little finger.

It was blue, because it was mostly made of water ice. I wish I had a more majestic descriptor, but there's not a better word for it: the blue was tipped in white and dusted with snow, but it was blue. Deep and sapphire and icy and... blue. And had more empty space than mass.

The Prismatic Moon was the oldest satellite of the Land Below, and it had endured hard abuse from asteroids at some point in its past. This was made obvious as you got closer: the satellite was made of porous ice, so when it was hit by debris it didn't form flat, round craters. Instead the rocks punched narrow and deep. It looked less like a celestial body than a frozen, half-exploded firework: walls and spikes of ice jutted out from a chilly, rocky core.

The Prism Witches had carved into these walls, shaping seven intricate towers from the abyss. As the ship drifted down I had a moment of panic—surely we'd crash!—but the space between the towers yawned and opened below us. The spires were clean and glassy, but not melting: I could see complicated images and shapes carved delicately into the ice. For a moment it was hard to discern what they were.

And then—a flash, a shift in the light, and magic happened. The images became clear as day, in full color, a huge, brilliant history of their moon. *Moving.* I glued my face to the window as I watched the first generation of Prism Witches direct light to shape the mountains, bore their homes into the ice, store their knowledge in scrolls of light...

There was a jolt. We had landed.

I tore myself away, suddenly embarrassed. Our tiny little village seemed unimpressive. Herschel must have been so underwhelmed. I was not prepared for this.

I took a deep breath, wrapped Herschel's gift around me tightly, and felt Pala's heart radiating warmth against mine, Esp's journal pressed against my chest. I could do this. It was going to be okay. They said I was the best choice, so I could do it. Breathe in. Breathe out.

The man wrapped in purple opened the door. I steeled my

spine and stepped outside, expecting a big crowd, like the one that had greeted Herschel on the Glottal Moon. Instead, I was met with three tall ladies, dressed in thick purple furs, and I was immediately handcuffed.

This was off to a *fantastic* start.

***

Inside the towers were labyrinthine halls and perplexing stairwells, and they wound me through these like a pet on a string. The floors were slick. Their pace was unforgiving.

The prison was cold.

I'd always assumed most prisons were cold, but this was a literal hole, carved in the ice. Iron bars, embedded in the floor and ceiling, kept me locked inside—there was a small silver gate, but it was fused to the iron and I didn't see how they worked it. The light was harsh and white, the air was cold and sterile. They'd let me keep my coat—and the gifts hidden inside it—because otherwise I'd probably freeze to death. I was immediately grateful for Pala's necklace.

The women were all as tall and white and blonde as Herschel. I couldn't tell them apart: their hoods were down, but they all wore the same violet, hooded mantle, the same long dress with the same ragged skirt. Same wool leggings. Same thick, spiked boots. The Prism Witches seemed to have a uniform.

"Is this how you treat all your students?" I asked, brushing the snow off my clothes. They'd been rough, dragging me here. "I thought I was here to learn!"

They ignored me. And left me there.

As soon as they were gone, I dug into my coat for Esp's journal—my parents would get me out of here. Even from a moon away. They'd burn down the entire ice moon if they had to. Pala and Esp would protect me. I could get help.

If only I had something to write with.

I rooted around in my coat for a minute or two, hoping for a miracle. Nothing showed up. I'd read stories about people writing sigils in their own blood, but I wasn't quite desperate enough for that yet. I had a lot of ice and therefore water, but if I used water I wasn't sure she'd be able to read my message, especially if it dried before she got to it.

Also, I didn't know what spell she'd used. For all I knew it only worked with ink. So now it was time for Plan B.

I circled the cell, taking in my surroundings. No windows. The door was welded to the bars. The rest of the cell was just... ice. I could barely walk. No visible guards, so... crazy thought, but maybe I could melt my way out?

I took Pala's necklace off and flicked open the heart. The little flame sparked and danced. I doubted I'd have enough time to melt a passage out of here, not with a flame this small, but maybe I could loosen a bar or two. With one final check of the hallways, I knelt, and pressed my locket against the floor.

At first I thought it was working—there was a wisp of steam and slow pocket of water formed. Pride blossomed in my chest. I was a genius. Except then I moved the flame, broadening the pocket... and whatever wasn't directly touched by fire froze again. Instantly.

Magic.

Okay, this wasn't going to work.

I got up, put my necklace back on, and paced for a while.

Fire was probably a useful tool to have here, but it wasn't going to melt the walls. I had the Bound Book, but no way to write in it. Maybe I could make charcoal from something I had on me? But again, I didn't know if she'd get that message...

Plus, if I did escape, what then? Freeze to death somewhere in the mountains?

There had to be *something*! I kicked the wall in frustration, lost my footing, and fell over.

Ow.

Someone laughed.

I sat up quickly. "Who's there?"

"Did you just fall over?" It was a boy's voice. Lazy and self-assured, almost teasing.

"Maybe." I fell back again, this time of my own free will. I didn't have the willpower to be upright. Everything was terrible. "What's it to you?"

"I did the same thing yesterday." He sounded muffled but close. Like he was right on the other side of the wall. "Tried to kick out the bars and fell over."

"Kick out the bars—like, escape?" I glanced at the site of my own attempt. Completely invisible now. I hadn't left a scratch.

"Yeah. It didn't work, though, they're in there deeper than they look."

"Yeah, I tried to melt my way out. Didn't work too well."

"Firestarter, huh? So is that what you're in for?"

"I don't even *know*. I don't think so, they don't know I can do that. I'm supposed to be an exchange student. I guess they don't trust me, but I don't know what they were expecting. We have one of *their* students…" my fingers played on the floor, tapping out an arrhythmic beat. "Not like they were talkative."

"I guess they wouldn't be. Sorry. I bet that's my fault."

"What did you do?"

"Came here to steal their secrets and undermine their government. So they might have figured you were gonna do the same thing. They don't actually know where I'm from, see."

"Great. Thanks a lot. Where *are* you from?"

"Wouldn't you like to know." I sat up again. *That* was cryptic. But before I could ask: "Wanna see something cool?"

"Huh?"

"Go stand in the far right corner," he said. "Away from me, away from the hall."

I was confused, but I did what he said. Was he a letter mage? His voice didn't sound familiar. Maybe he was from one of the other moons?

There were some shuffling noises. The cell exploded.

With a blast of steam and a concussive shot, I was knocked off my feet for the third time today. For a second I could hear *nothing*—this was a small, enclosed space, and I'd learned something new: explosions were *loud*. Really loud. Much louder than they'd seemed when I heard military drills back home. Much louder than the hum of a sinocycle's gun. When my hearing returned, my ears were ringing.

I was okay otherwise. Nothing major blew up in my direction—some hot water, which hit my coat, and some steam, which made me cough. It clouded the room for a moment, and when it cleared, I could see my new friend.

He was a little taller than me, handsome and slight. His skin was lighter than mine, but it wasn't anywhere near as pale as the Prism Witches, or even Pala's. More of a warm brown, a tint that suggested sunlight in his genes. His smile suggested sunlight too, but I couldn't pin down what about it made that comparison.

Brightness, maybe.

He was wrapped in what looked like several layers of warmer-weather clothing, impromptu winter wear, and his eyes were obscured by a pair of beetle-like viridian goggles. His leather vest (atop the layered shirts) was ornamented with various vials and gearish amalgamations—how had he kept those? I hadn't been searched too thoroughly, but I *had* been searched. They clearly weren't decorative. He'd just blown up the jail.

His hair was black and wild, highlighted with streaks of vivid green.

He was my age. Maybe a little younger. I wasn't expecting that. He spoke like an adult, confident and self-assured. And despite the goggles, he clearly wasn't one of the men I'd seen here. He spoke, for one thing.

"Hey," he said, and held out his hand like we were meeting at a party or something. "Welcome to the Prismatic College."

I shook his hand. "Uh, nice to meet you. I'm Aleph. And you are-"

There was a sudden and distinct sound of hastily-approaching footsteps. "On the run," said the boy, and he grabbed my hand. "This way!"

I scrambled to keep up with him, mind racing. This was a huge turn of events, and not one I was necessarily happy about. Esp hadn't asked me to run away with a mysterious green-haired boy, she'd asked me to observe and learn about the Prism Witches. I didn't know who he was, what he'd done, or if Esp would want information on him too. Or even if I wanted to be his friend.

But I ran with him.

Straight into a crowd of *true* Prismatic men, faces all covered in colored wrappings. We skidded to a halt, sliding a bit on the ice floor, and my new friend looked around for an opening. Without asking permission, he promptly flung both of us through the nearest window.

***

It was open. In the frigid, inhospitable air, the window was open. So we didn't have to worry about breaking the glass, but the thousand-foot fall into the abyss was another story. For the third time in the past few weeks, I stared down my death. I held the mystery boy's hand tightly and froze, preparing to die in the void.

But my new friend had other plans. In a swift, fluid motion, he twisted, pulled a small spear-gun from a pocket (how did he still *have that?*), aimed it at the ice tower, and fired. It hit its mark and stuck tight, trailing a long cord that disappeared into his vest. Still falling, the boy grabbed the cord with one leather-gloved hand and pulled me close to his side with the other. I held on instinctively.

He smelled sharply of kerosene and lavender.

The rope pulled taut and we *sprung* upwards, the cord coiling into a mechanism on the boy's side. We lost momentum rapidly, but for a moment we were flying. I could see the moving pictures refracted on the ice walls, and we were suspended in a chasm of light and color. It was beautiful. Way better than the view from the ship.

And then we landed, lightly, on a ledge far above the spot we'd jumped from. I wavered and nearly fell a second time, but he kept me upright. It took me a second to realize we were still alive. And then: "What in the *world* was that?"

He grinned at me. "I got you out of prison."

"You *broke* me out of prison."

"I wasn't aware there's a difference." He was surprisingly nonchalant for someone who'd just base-jumped out of a tower. The boy edged along the glassy mural, careful of his feet. I followed him. The lights danced around us, flashing from a thousand different non-specific sources. We were moving carefully inside the images that painted the outside of the towers.

It was a good camouflage, but it had a biting wind. Indoors had been cold, but outdoors was *freezing.* The dryness of the air caught in my lungs.

"Believe me," I said, "there's a difference. From the cell I could have earned their trust and learned from them like I was *supposed* to, and now they're gonna think I'm on your side! I don't even know what your side is!"

"My side is *my* side," he said. "I'm supposed to learn here too, you know. Figure out what the heck is going on up here."

"Up here? What moon are you *from?*"

There was a flash of bright, *bright* light, and suddenly our spot on the wall was illuminated. Scratch that, everything was illuminated—they'd turned off the moving murals, and all seven towers were suddenly, blindingly white.

The boy grabbed my hand again and dragged me along the ledge. "My ship's down at the bottom. If we get to it, we can get away and back home, and I can let my father know what I know."

"We?" I struggled to keep up. His boots handled the slippery ledge better than mine, and he was moving quickly. I didn't want to fall again.

"Unless you'd rather be with *them*," he said, nodding at a group of sinocycles that were suddenly zooming toward us.

"The monks—"

"The witches," he corrected me. "They have these small ships—"

"Sinocycles. Those are Fourier Monk technology. They must trade." That was odd. *No one* traded with the Monks, I thought. More information for Esp. I slowed down for a moment to get a good look, which must have annoyed my new friend—he physically tugged me through another open window.

"Stop *looking*, they'll get you!"

"But they shouldn't have—"

"Aleph, *we're on the run.* Not taking notes on a field trip. C'mon, this way."

Speak for yourself, I thought, but I followed him. "Where are we going? We're not trying to leave the towers, are we? We'll die out there."

"I'm looking for the elevator they took me up in. There's one that goes straight to the hangar and then we can get my ship."

Okay.

"I think it's—" He skidded to a stop and kicked open a door. That seemed a little excessive. They wouldn't be locked out *here.* "Yes! Through here!"

Hallway. Metal grated doors revealed an elevator across from us. They were already open, so he didn't have to kick these down—just cranked them shut behind us. He bound them together with another small device—a metal rod that expanded and hooked them together, keeping them closed—and down we went.

Quickly.

"Listen," said the boy, "I'm sorry I broke you out of jail without your permission. But I promise you, you don't want to be stuck under their, um, questioning. I did you a huge favor. You can still get the answers you're supposed to get. I promise, we're on the same side."

"You said you were on *your* side."

"Well yeah, but we have the same goal, right? Information. I need to figure out if this place is a threat. I want to keep the peace. Isn't that why you're here too?"

I thought about the sinocycle that tried to kidnap me. About Esp insisting that I report to her and only her. It hadn't really been clear. The whole idea of *threat* was nebulous and undefined. "Maybe," I said. "I think we're trying to foster *trust* between the schools, though. This isn't very trustworthy behavior."

"Please," said the mystery boy. "No one on the moons can handle trust."

"What do you mean, *on the moons*?" I was all for political commentary and everything, but that seemed a little extreme.

"I'll explain everything when we get to my father. Promise."

***

The elevator grounded in a long hallway, which led out to an open hangar. The ceiling here sloped away into the sky, allowing the free ingress and egress of the local vessels. The boy dragged me to the end of a row of cargo freighters, making a straight shot.

I could tell which ship was his from here. It wasn't a freighter, for one, just a little island-hopper. It was small. It matched the boy's aesthetic, lots of brassy plates and a viridian cabin window.

Also, it was terrible.

I lived on a moon: I knew what spaceships looked like. This did not look like a spaceship. It looked like something a kid threw together in his backyard. A glance at my new friend made me wonder if it *had* been thrown together in his backyard. I wasn't trusting this thing in the vacuum of space. I wasn't even sure I wanted to *go* with him—he hadn't even given me his name.

I paused. "Can this thing even *fly*?"

"It can fly *fine*," said the boy, reaching for my arm. "Come on, we don't have much time—"

"It doesn't even look like a spaceship!"

"It looks fine!" There was a commotion down the hallway. People were getting closer. The boy opened a door and scrambled into the cockpit. "Come on, Aleph, get in-"

I could see a future stretched out before me: what would happen if I got into the ship. He'd take me to his father. Explain what was going on. I'd probably wind up a rebel of some time. That future didn't have the Glottal Moon in it. Or Esp and Pala. Or Annie. It was an exciting life, maybe, of being on the run and… getting whatever information he was trying to get, but it didn't have home.

And I didn't know this guy.

"No."

"What?"

"No! I didn't ask for any of this—"

There's one thing I'll never forget about that moment, more than the consequences of my decision. The look on the boy's face was sad—impossibly, disproportionately sad. Not angry. Hurt. And for a split second I wondered what would happen if I got in anyway.

And then he closed the door, right as the others closed in on us. There were loud demands made at impossible volumes: "LAND AT ONCE" and "YOU ARE UNDER ARREST" and "SURRENDER IMMEDIATELY", but the boy didn't listen to them. Something about him told me he didn't listen to anyone.

His ship powered up with a great hum, and I bolted. In a synchronized motion, the Prism Witches and covered men turned away and shielded themselves. There was a roar like an escaping animal. There was bright, green light. There was a great, burning wind.

When I looked back the boy's ship was far above us, bright as a coin under the sun.

THE LOW JAIL'S
WARDEN
-interlude-

Ingress didn't call her in often. That was all right: Esp didn't like him much. They'd known each other for years. She felt safe in saying he was weak, unintelligent, and nowhere near as inspiring as he thought he was.

But he was the High Linguist, and he'd called her in. He wanted a meeting. So Esp went, and sat in front of him, and waited for the man to get to the point.

"I thought we could have a chat about the prisoner."

"He's not saying much," said Esp. "Nothing new."

"I thought we could have a chat about how you're *treating* the prisoner," Ingress said.

"Three meals a day, a place to sleep, and a place to relieve himself. Better treatment than I got."

Ingress sighed. "So you're aware of the rumors."

"The rumors can kiss my—"

"Esp, it's understandable. He tried to kidnap your son. You're an aggressive woman, and you can be impulsive. I know you lost your temper with Resh yesterday."

"He wanted to take the man to the High Prison. I didn't lose my temper, I just don't trust—"

"Resh was acting on my orders, Esperint. The prisoner will be moved today. I'm asking you to take some time off from the Low Jail. I know you're upset, but you don't need to get hysterical."

Esp clenched her fists. Ingress was too oblivious to appreciate her self-restraint.

THE
VIRIDIAN BOY

-4-

There was no sunlight in here.

An odd, manufactured beam illuminated me from an undefined point on the ceiling, casting glinting shadows across the room. The walls were white, intricately carved, with blue sinking through their corners. They were freezing to the touch, but never slick—ice didn't seem to melt logically inside the spires.

If it did, I'd have melted a hollow in the table by now. My body was uncomfortably pressed up against it. And my chair would be long gone. But beneath the fur covering, the chair didn't even feel cold.

A tall woman stood across from me, paying more attention to the scroll in her hands than to her prisoner. She was a Violet— the mantle around her shoulders was purple. I thought it was the same long-nosed one that had thrown me in prison, but it was hard to be sure. All the blond-haired, white-skinned ladies looked the same to me.

"Did you assist in his escape?" Her tone was commanding. Confusing. She didn't seem actively hostile, but I was definitely in trouble. If I played along, maybe she'd let me go.

I'd been playing along for hours.

"No." I kept my eyes glued to the table. My heart was pounding. I'd made my choice: now I needed to see it through. If I'd wanted something easy, I'd have gone with the boy who indirectly put me here. "He broke us both out, dragged me with him, and then I refused to leave on his ship."

"Do you know who he is?"

"No," I said. "He wouldn't tell me."

She was quiet for a moment, tracing her finger along the scroll. I'd never seen one before, but I'd heard about them: the light scrolls of the Prism Witches. One piece of paper (or vellum, I guess, or parchment, or *something*) that had access to the entire library. All the knowledge of the world in the palm of your hand. It sparked a little. I could see the imprints of letters on the parchment, but there was nothing I could make out properly. They shifted and cracked like floes on a frozen river.

"You're scared of me," she said.

"Yes."

"Well, you're honest, for a boy. That's something." The woman smirked. "Aleph Worf-Sapir, was it?"

"Yes."

"My name is Maiman Williams." She waved her hand and the spotlight widened, dimmed, and filled the room. I blinked in the sudden change of atmosphere.

"Williams? You're Herschel's mom."

"I used to be Herschel's guardian. I am not her mother." Maiman pulled a chair from somewhere behind me and sat, facing me across the table. "It's all right, Aleph. You can relax. You're not in trouble."

I looked down at my bound hands. "I feel like I'm in trouble."

"You're not in trouble *anymore*. We needed to assess the situation. We needed to know what he'd told you and whether or not you'd believed him. Fortunately you're a smart young man, Aleph." She smiled at me again. I wasn't sure what to think of that —it was kind of a patronizing expression. But I smiled back carefully. I didn't know how to read her yet.

"What was I supposed to not believe? Who was that?"

"Someone very dangerous." Maiman sighed. "His name is Alexander Normal, and he's a child spy from the Land Below. His father is their global minister of security. Apparently sent his son to check in on us. We're not sure what aroused *his* suspicion, but since the exchange program was suggested shortly after his arrival you can understand ours."

Esp and I had had a lot of conversations about gut feelings. She was always a big believer in intuition, that your gut saw things your eyes could miss. Right now, my gut was thinking about Alexander's smile. How it had brightened the room. Maiman's didn't meet her eyes. Granted, Alexander had busted me out of jail and asked me to betray my people. I tucked the feeling away to think about later.

A note from the future: I should have listened to my gut.

"So why do you trust me now?"

"Well, we didn't put you under the Light just to intimidate

you," Maiman said. "When we have questions to ask, we can use the Light to check your vital signs when you answer. I read your pulse. Like I said, you were honest with me."

"Then can you untie me?"

***

She didn't untie me. She walked me through the halls at a brisk pace, barely giving me time to look around or get my bearings. Esp have told me that they were keeping me disoriented on purpose, so I'd be reliant on them. It was a control thing. My mother was knowledgeable about tricks like that.

I couldn't do anything about it, but I was aware. Aware meant I could do something about it in the future.

It was night now—the windows, still unimaginably *open*, were dark, reflecting only the light show outside. From my glimpses into the night, I could still see the moving murals against the spires. They were clearer from here than they had been from the ship when I'd arrived.

"Where are we going?" I asked, trying yet again to balance speed with staying upright. Why did everyone in the Prismatic College move so *fast*?

"You'll be staying with me while you're here," Maiman said. She didn't look at me. "In Herschel's old room. Your things have already been brought in."

"Thank you," I said. I had nothing to be actually grateful for, but she seemed to expect it anyway. "And I'll get the chance to study?"

"Your department informed me that you'll have work to do for your own studies while you're here, so you'll be provided a room in one of the Violet Libraries to do so in the afternoons. As you'll be unsupervised you will not be allowed to *leave* that room, but I'll have a man on post to get you whatever you may need. In the mornings you'll study with me, and occasionally join the Reds for basic lessons."

I should have expected that. According to Herschel, Reds were children. Usually younger than eleven. They were also undoubtedly already better than me at light magic, since I wasn't even sure what light magic *was*, so that was going to be fun.

"Thank you for your investment, Maiman."

"To you," said Maiman, "I am Violet Master Maiman, or simply Violet. You may call me Violet Maiman if we are in the presence of other Violets and you need to distinguish. Are we clear?"

"Yes, Violet."

"Good." She stopped at an elevator and let me go in first. We rode in silence for a few seconds.

It opened into a courtyard.

We were indoors, but there wasn't a better word for the space—it was covered in plants. There was a water fountain (carved in curling spirals from ice—how did that *work*? Shouldn't something melt? Or freeze?) and a circular path around it, mercifully paved with dark pebbles. Blue-green grasses with electric, amethyst flowers crowded up around statues of Prism Witches. The ceiling arched above us, lined with delicate, filigree buttresses that draped arctic willow through the air.

It was cool in here but humid, and everything was kissed with frost.

Ten wood doors and a hallway spread out before us. The statues lined up with them—a permanent form of name card, I guessed. Each woman was dressed in the usual Prism Witch furs and heavy boots, with ragged hems and heavy hoods. They were in differing poses with differing accessories: crystalline roses with icicle thorns, a hawk, an open book...

It was a little creepy. The room was *silent*, except for the pouring of water. Even Maiman didn't make a sound as she strode to the nearest door—up a path framed with slender, white-flowered tea bushes—and through it.

I realized this was where she *lived*. This was where *Herschel* had lived. Our house wasn't small by any standards, but it had never been this glamorous. Even the High Linguist's tower wasn't this intricate.

I stumbled in behind her. My footsteps crunched on little bubbles of ice between the paving-stones. I sounded like a giant.

Maiman's home was a little more spartan. The same black stones paved her rooms, the same plants cascaded from her walls. Clear, glassy ice had been shaped into furniture—slanting chairs, filigree counters, low tables—while the hard white stuff formed the outer walls. Glacial, deep blue slabs made low dividing barriers. The latter blocked off a small kitchenette in the center of the living area: a dark wood counter and a ventilated fire pit, a curved stone in an ice cradle.

Wood was an expensive luxury at home, but this moon had spots of tundra. I wasn't sure whether it was rare here or not. With the exception of the fire pit, everything was made of ice, fur, and that same dark wood.

It was beautiful. But it lacked ornamentation: there were no paintings on the walls, no photographs of her and Herschel, no *art* of any kind. The walls were carved in geometric patterns, but they were bare. Pala would have cried. Instinctively I touched the necklace she'd given me.

Maiman shed her outer cloak and waved her hand in the direction of the pit—it sparked to life. Another wave of the hand and the ropes around my wrists hissed and burned away.

I pretended not to be impressed.

"Your rooms are that way. I'll bring you some dinner in a moment. Go get comfortable." Maiman paused. "In return for our hospitality, I would appreciate it if you shared any information you have on Alexander Normal."

I felt Esp's book pressing against my chest.

"Anything you need, ma'am. I wish I had more, but he didn't talk much."

***

My bags were there. They were a little worse for the wear and not in the same state as when I'd packed them—I was sure they'd been thoroughly searched—but they were there.

They were unceremoniously piled in one corner of the room. There was furniture: a truly massive pile of pelts atop a shelf in an alcove made her bed, and her desk was inset with polished mahogany. Complete with matching chair. There was a window, but it looked out away from the other towers, into the blackness of the Prismatic Moon.

Herschel's room. It looked like Herschel. No wonder it was a bit showy.

Whoever had cleaned it last—I assumed Herschel herself— they hadn't expended much effort. Piles of books obscured the corners that weren't occupied by my luggage, odd crystalline structures had stacked up unceremoniously at the back of her desk, incomprehensible sketches were tacked to the walls. Most of the sketches had something to do with prism magic, I guessed— lots of math and angles and numbers. A few made me feel a little more at home.

Herschel was a decent sketch artist. There were some cross-hatchings of tundra plants scattered around her walls, some pencil drawings of arctic foxes. I ran my fingers over a scientifically-accurate sketch of tea flowers, fascinated, before I saw the only portrait in the room. It was hidden, low on the wall where it couldn't be seen from the door. The paper was a little more crinkled than the other pictures, and it had clearly been touched up a few times.

I recognized the face.

Maiman.

Herschel clearly hadn't been the one to pick up, then. I wasn't sure if she would have taken the picture with her, burned it, or hidden it, but there was no way she'd want anyone to see this. Much less myself *and* the five other students who'd be staying here. I removed the picture carefully and put it in Esp's journal. I'd get it back to her later.

I was tired, but before anything else I wanted to check in. It was hard to believe that the last time I'd slept, I'd slept at home— already it felt like I'd been gone for months.

There was a note waiting for me.

If the reader of these words is not my son, give the kid his journal back.

Aleph,

Pala and I love you. Write when you have time. Remember to do your lessons.

These may be good people. But they are people. *They aren't your friends.*

Remember that you're working at cross purposes.

Esp

Mom,

Love you too. It's been an interesting past 24 hours. I got arrested! But not maliciously. It looks like there were some unrelated security concerns. I met a spy from the Land Below. Alexander Normal. Sound familiar to you?

Miss home terribly. Can't wait to be back. Excited to learn prism magic tomorrow, though.
Love you,
Aleph

And with that done I fell into Herschel's bed, and instantly went to sleep.

***

The Red classroom was shorter than me. So were all the Reds. At fourteen I hadn't hit my growth spurt yet, but I was big enough to feel awkward in a classroom sized for eight-year-olds. I walked in, took one look at the long, short tables, and my knees hurt preemptively. There was already a group of small girls standing in the back, and they all stared at me. Memories of my early days in the Lower College came rushing back.

"Uh, hi?"

"Is that *him*?" one whispered to her friend, staring. "Why is he so dark?" They were all blue-eyed, pale-skinned, yellow-haired. I felt bizarrely self-conscious. Wrong gender, wrong age, wrong *color*. I'd never been so out of place.

Someone cleared her throat behind me. I stepped aside to let a Verde through. She was barely older than me. She was a kid too.

"Aleph Worf-Sapir?"

"Yeah. Yes. Um. Hi."

"Good to meet you. I'm Lee Gödel, I'm their instructor. Go ahead and set your things in the back. I'm afraid we'll have you standing, I don't want to have you distracting the girls. And a taller desk should suit you better anyway, I'll have one in for you next time."

"Thanks," I said, unsure again why I felt pressured to be grateful. I stood in the back of the room and waited as the rest of the kids filed in. They each greeted me with a stare and silence. No questions, no introductions. I couldn't *quite* blame them for it. Herschel had faced a crowd too.

"Tell me about the Light," said Lee. It was clearly a cue of some kind. The girls immediately rushed to their chairs and sat, facing forward. "What is the first law?"

"The Light is a true connection," said thirty small voices in unison.

"What is the second?"

"The Light stores all we know," they replied.

"What is the third?"

"Any person can access the Light." With the third law, a few curious faces glanced back at me. I stayed quiet. We had three laws of magic too, rules they taught us back in the Low College, but we didn't recite them before class.

"As you've noticed," said Lee, "we have a new student with us today. Aleph Worf-Sapir is a Letter Mage from the Glottal Moon. He's going to observe us occasionally for the next month while we practice summoning and literacy."

"Observe?" I didn't realize I'd asked it aloud until every eye in the room was on me. "I thought I was here to learn."

Giggles.

Lee smiled apologetically. "Men can't summon the Light," she said. "You're welcome to try, of course, but there are biological differences."

"Biological differences?"

A small voice piped up. "Men are slaves to base desires!"

"Language, Presper," said Lee. "But yes. Biological differences. I'm going to have to ask you to be quiet, Aleph, the girls need to focus."

The girls were given an assignment: practice summoning for a few minutes. Lee put on some quiet music and the girls all laid their hands out on their tables, open and cupped. There was a silence of intense concentration.

I was quiet, but my mind was spinning. I'd learned to expect the patronizing tone from Prism Witches, but somehow having it come from children made it sting more. I didn't want to just sit and watch this. I was here to learn.

I counted as a person.

Fuming, I cupped my hands in the air and tried to figure out what they were doing. They were concentrating hard—but on what? For what result? Summoning the Light, I assumed, but what the heck did that look like? A sunbeam? Or a scroll?

The girl who'd called me base—Presper—helped me out. She was the first to be successful. Something above her hands sparked and flashed—I heard a static crackle, and she laughed. Lee gave her an approving smile.

Okay. So that was what it looked like. So how had she *done* it?

I went over what I knew of Light Magic: it could be used to store information in the scrolls. It looked way too dangerous for an eight-year-old girl to have stored in her hands. And the Laws. Somehow I should be able to figure out what, physically, I was supposed to do.

Try as I might, though, nothing sparked in my hands.

***

It was a tough morning.

Maiman came and got me before I could escape to the room they'd set aside. I wanted to be alone: embarrassingly, I wanted to cry. But she didn't get to know that.

"We're going to have an afternoon lesson today, and you can continue your letter studies tomorrow," she told me, and whisked me off before I could protest.

The seven ice spires housed Prism Witches at various levels of study: the Red spire hosted the Reds, the Alani spire hosted the Alani, and so on. As they reached the upper limits of their abilities, the spires' population dropped: very few made it to Violet, and many never progressed beyond Verde. An extreme few, with various intellectual challenges, never made it beyond Red.

To the Prism Witches' credit, the adult Red women were treated with respect. A few picked up some struggling students in my class for tutoring. They'd have been treated with disdain back home on the Glottal Moon. Here they were greeted with smiles and embraces.

The Witches were clearly *capable* of empathy. I just wasn't seeing any of it.

As their populations dwindled, the size of each spire's library grew: the Reds had half a floor's worth of light scrolls. The Violet Library spanned ten stories. This was where we were headed: a huge space with hardly anyone to be seen. As we entered, the stacks peeled away around us like a blossoming rose, and the ground floor opened before us.

The stacks rippled away from a central lift in great rings, light scrolls softly glowing in their nooks. The Scrolls were *almost* quiet. A quiet background static betrayed their life. Around us, the library walls lifted away and arched into a clouded glass ceiling. Silent shadows marked the presence of witches on the floor above.

It was beautiful.

The room itself was filled with Light. Light-as-a-proper-noun, not just stuff filtering in from the windows outside: it shifted, changed, pulsed as Prism Witches all over the moon accessed the data stored there.

Directly in front of the entry door was a great cerulean crystal. It was impossible to miss: it was roughly the size of my desk at home, held in a frame of silver, flickering with letters and shapes across its flat surface, and glowing. Like, really glowing. It lit up the room.

Maiman approached the crystal and tapped its surface. A map appeared on the surface as if sketched from some internal source. I pretended not to be impressed again: that would be incredibly useful for letter magic.

"This is the Terminal. During your studies you may need to find a scroll or some information, and since you will not be capable of summoning the scrolls or the Light, you'll need to ask someone to help you use this."

"Thanks," I said.

"Study C is available right now. We'll go in there."

***

The door was barely closed before my question escaped. "Why won't you teach me?"

Maiman sighed.

"I'm here to learn. I'm supposed to be learning *prism magic*, not just standing in the back of the classroom watching a bunch of kids make pretty lights. This isn't right."

"I know," said Maiman.

"I just think—you do?" I was caught off-guard. I couldn't read Maiman. One second she seemed half-decent, one second she refused to untie my wrists. I had an idea of how poorly she'd treated Herschel, and I knew I needed to be wary. But she was also the closest thing I had to an ally here. And even if she'd treated Herschel poorly, the girl clearly loved her for *some* reason. "Why?"

"We weren't expecting a boy," said Maiman, taking a seat

and removing a Scroll from her bag. "Silly of us, we know the other university moons don't quite understand, but it still caught us by surprise."

That sort of answered my questions. I remembered how Herschel had first treated *me,* too. "What does that have to do with anything?"

"Men can't do prism magic," said Maiman. "Even one raised by two women. Did the girls say their Three Rules when you were in their class this morning?"

"Yes?"

"Do you remember them?"

"The Light is a true connection. To access the Light is to command all knowledge. Any person can access the Light."

"Exactly. Any person."

I'm not sure why I asked. Their position was pretty clear. I guess I had to hear her say it. "Am I not a person?"

"There have been long sequestrations among the Violets on the topic, Aleph, and many discussions of both a scientific and ethical nature. And while you are human—let no one tell you otherwise—the consensus is that no, you are not a whole person."

"*Excuse me?*"

"A person in the eyes of the Light is a creature with a single, complete soul. A woman has a complete soul. She has the gift to create life and use the Light. A man does not. A man's soul is a fraction of the whole, designed to meet with a woman's and fracture her power."

I did not have words. Esp would have hit her by now. *Pala* would have hit her by now, and she had much higher standards for physical violence.

"Because of this, men cannot create life, and they cannot use the Light. A woman summons by connecting to the love of their sisters. Men, by definition, cannot feel the connection to their sisters. So trying to teach you prism magic is like trying to cup water in your skirts, Aleph. Usually it all spills and you've wasted the water, and if it holds you've ruined the vessel and the water leaks away regardless. Don't take it personally."

I remembered Esp's words. *These people aren't my friends.*

"Thank you for being so accommodating, Violet." Gratitude was starting to feel vulgar.

"You're welcome, Aleph. So instead, we're going to study

theory. We'll give you the tools to take something back to your women."

***

They were wrong. Maiman and Lee and Presper, they were *wrong*. I *knew* they were wrong. They had to be.

That evening I sat in the darkness, hands cupped, trying to feel that connection. To feel love, to feel friendship, to feel *something*. It seemed impossible. I couldn't connect with them. I didn't know them. And they hated me.

I missed my family. I missed being around people who didn't hate me for no reason. I even missed the bickering—the Master of Letters with his pompous nonsense and Esp's constant frustration with the administration—

Something clicked.

Maybe I didn't need a connection to the witches. Maybe I just needed a connection. I stopped trying to focus on Herschel, and instead thought about my family. I hadn't written to them again, not tonight. I missed them. I missed the fire garden and Pala's cooking. I missed Esp's quiet advice. I thought about their faces, and their voices, and the last times I'd hugged them. And then I thought about—

There was a spark.

I jolted upright in bed, heart pounding. I'd seen it. A flash of light, small but clear and warm. I'd done it. I'd *felt* it. And of course I'd managed to summon it alone, in my room, with no one there to see. But maybe I could do it again. With Maiman there to witness it.

There was a tap on the window. I glanced up—a shadow, small and hunched, was sitting on the ledge outside. For some ridiculous reason I nearly summoned the Light again.

Alexander.

I didn't rush. I got out of bed and put on my slippers, walked slowly to the window, opened it warily. I didn't think he'd kill me: I was *supposed* to see him as a threat. I had to be on guard. He was dangerous. But he looked cold out there.

We froze for a moment, staring at each other. He looked about ready to bolt. I briefly considered pushing him off the tower. I didn't know why he was here, and he didn't know what I was about to do. But he'd tapped. He wanted to talk to me.

And I didn't have any real desire to hurt him.

I stepped back. "What are you *doing*? You left!"

"What were *you* doing? You stayed!" From this close, I could see him shivering. He jumped inside and closed the window behind him, even though open air didn't seem to cool the towers at all. He'd been wearing a heavy coat and those ridiculously green glasses. Now he removed them, hanging both on the back of Herschel's chair.

"Careful— those are covered in snow, the wood—" He looked at me like I was crazy. "Listen, I don't know what it's like down on the planet, but this stuff's rare up here."

He laughed. "So they told you, huh? I'm from the homeland." Alexander moved his dripping, snowy coat to the floor next to the windowsill. His goggles stayed in his hand. "I'm a dangerous spy sent from the planet to come destroy you all. Well, there goes my big mysterious reveal."

"How disappointing for you."

"I'm heartbroken." Alexander shot me another smile, but this one didn't brighten the room. He was worried about something. It was a little concerning that I could read him so easily. "You spoiled everything, my friend."

"Oh, we're friends, huh?" That came out less sarcastically than I'd meant. He was right. We were friends. I didn't know why. There was literally no reason to trust the guy. He was attractive, and easygoing, but he didn't have much else going for him.

But I liked him. For whatever reason. Maybe because he'd trusted me first. I relented. "Why in the world are you here?"

"Maybe I missed you." He winked. My heart had a brief, infuriating reaction, but I ignored it. He was teasing me. No one risked their lives for a missed connection. My eyes held his steadily, and Alexander sighed. He slumped down into the bed. "I need your help."

"That seems like a terrible reason to show up in my bedroom in the middle of the night." He froze for a moment, then laughed again. I felt my ears redden. "*You know what I mean.*"

"I know, I know—I mean, it's not like you were sleeping—"

"Wait, were you *watching* me?"

"What? No! I mean—a little, but not like *that*—"

"Why were you watching me sleep?" I grinned.

"Will you *be quiet*? Maiman's in the other room—"

"Oh, were you watching her sleep too?"

Alexander threw a pelt at me. "Shut up!"

"Do you just watch *everyone* sleep?" I threw it back and sat next to him. "You have *no* reason to trust me."

"Sure I do. You didn't sound the alarm when you saw me in the window."

"And when you *came* to the window?" Suspicious. I was supposed to be suspicious.

"Put it this way. I don't trust you a *lot* less than I don't trust them. And like I said, I need your help. I don't really have an alternative."

"I'm waiting."

"They messed with my ship. The second I hit low orbit, my computers just freaked out. Sending signals in every direction possible, set a trajectory to send me right back to the hangar. I managed to cut off whatever malware they loaded me up with, but I don't know what it sent them before I deleted it."

"Okay?" I had no idea what I had to do with any of this.

"I need to sneak into the Violet Library and get rid of whatever information they logged."

"And you need me for that? Because I really don't know much about light magic. I don't know how much help I'm gonna be."

Alexander stood up, stretching. Without the coat and the belts, he was a little scrawny. A little underfed. "Nah, I can handle that. I was originally planning to be in and out with no help at all. The problem is, your writing system is totally different from back home. I can press buttons all I like, but I can't *read*." He grinned back down at me, and *now* it felt real. He looked less worried. His eyes were as green as his goggles. "I'm guessing you know a lot about that, Letter Mage."

"I do."

"You can tell them I was here if you want, I don't care. Just give me a chance to get out. Please."

"It's fine," I said, standing next to him. If it wasn't public, if no one saw me helping him, nothing was jeopardized. "No one needs to know."

He relaxed.

"Let's go save your ship," I said, grabbing Herschel's gift

and a real pair of shoes. Alexander retrieved his coat. "I mean, if that's the right word for it. Would you *call* it a ship?"

***

The Masters' Dormitory was on the tenth floor, and the terminal was on the ground. We had a long way down, and a lift wasn't a possibility. They were convenient, but loud, and would require sneaking past Maiman.

One of Alexander's little harpoons was embedded in the wall outside my window—a conveniently dark place. The prismatic displays weren't in place on this side of the spire. Who would see them?

Alexander hooked his belt to the rope hanging from the harpoon and pulled a pair of rough gloves from the pockets of his coat. He glanced over at me. "We're gonna rappel down side by side. How much do you weigh?"

I told him.

"Okay, lucky, we're about the same weight. My coat should make up for most of the slack. See how the rope's tied here? I've got one clip on my belt, and I'll have to do a makeshift harness for you, but then we'll go down. Descend in sync. Shouldn't be too tough."

I looked at the long way down. We were standing on packed snow, not solid ice, but I didn't want to get close to the edge just in case.

"Don't give me that, we'll be fine." Alexander dragged some cord out of another pocket—how many pockets did he have?—and began to fiddle. "Look straight down—the levels are stacked, see? That's the ledge we're standing on now. Each floor is a little smaller than the one below it. If we fall, unless we're really unlucky, we won't go the whole way down."

"Like we did last time," I said. I was only half-teasing. That had been terrible. I was learning to hate heights.

"Like we did last time." Alexander nudged me. "Do I know how to do a first date or what?"

"A *what*?"

"Here, put this on." He tossed me something. It looked like underwear made of rope. "And follow my lead."

***

We landed in front of the doors, which were impressive. The towers stretched above us, scraping the stars. Wind whipped and wound between them, fluttering against our bodies. It wasn't as biting as it had been earlier—the weather had calmed, or maybe I was just a little more prepared. We stood close, looking up at where we'd come from. We'd just climbed *down* that.

Alexander pressed a button on his jacket. The line went slack as the arrow received a signal, ten stories above us, and he tugged it down to store back on his person. Guess I wasn't getting back up that way.

The doors were locked, these great black gates. I had no idea how to open them. Last time I'd been here, they'd already been open. Surely Alexander didn't expect more luck with windows.

I glanced over at my friend and he looked back, clearly expecting something. "It needs the Light," he said. "Prism Witches shine their Light on the door and it opens."

"What? I told you, I'm not a Prism Witch. I can't—"

"I saw you do it. How'd you do it before?"

I hoped he'd attribute the color of my face to the wind. "I don't know. The Light's about human connection, relationships. Somehow. I was just thinking about my family and—" Heh. "And people. And suddenly it happened."

"Well, try." He flashed me a smile again. "Think about whichever people spark that human connection."

"I've only done it once." I raised my hands in a cup, like the Reds did in Lee's class, like an offering to the gateway before me. I closed my eyes, breathed deep. Let myself relax into the moment, ignored everything around me, and just felt my love for my family. For my friends.

Nothing happened.

I exhaled. I opened my eyes. I saw Alexander—face mostly obscured, but body language betraying a hint of incomprehensible disappointment. And the Light flared in my hands. Just a spark, like before, but enough to open the door.

I pushed inside, out of the cold, before I could see the look on his face. Idiot.

Wait.

"You said you knew what you were doing. How did you get in here earlier without the Light?"

"Oh, yeah. It doesn't have to be Light-with-a-capital-L. I just used my flashlight the first time I got in here. Once you get to the dirt their security is *atrocious.*"

"So what was the purpose of that whole challenge, then?"

"I wanted to see how you did it." Alexander unzipped his coat as we got inside and pushed up his goggles. I was fine—a little warm, but not uncomfortable. Alexander gave the impression that he hated wearing winter gear.

The Violet Library wasn't dark, but the lights were off. Our path to the terminal was lit by the light scrolls and their low, static hum: the effect was that of a glacially-slow kaleidoscope. Colors were cast in shifting patterns against the shadows on the floor. The only stable light in the room came from the terminal itself.

I leaned over it.

"So what does it say?" Alexander asked.

"It says a lot of stuff. 'Catalog', 'Search', 'Enter Data', 'New Data'..."

"New data. Let's try that one."

Going off what I'd seen from Maiman, I reached out and pressed my fingers to the crystal over the words "New Data". The crystal didn't give way or budge at all, but the light shimmered out from my hands like a ripple on a pond. A new menu came up, *far* more comprehensive than the last one—lines and lines of text— but I had a suspicion. A little blinking diamond drew my attention to a line at the very top.

"The line by the diamond says 'INPUT NEEDED MACEDONIA 8', is that you?"

"Macedonia 8. That's my ship, yeah." Alexander tapped it for me.

"Eight? What happened to the first seven?"

"Shut up." He was looking intently at the new screen. "What does it say?"

"Uh... There's a lot of it. Lots of stuff about operating systems and... words I don't really understand. I think these are engine specs—it says Eon Drive? Did you name all these yourself? You *built* this thing, right?"

"Maybe. But a lot of this is my dad's tech. It can't get into their hands." He paused for a second. "...I guess I can't tell you not to read this stuff."

"That's literally what I'm here for, so no. Want me to get rid of it?"

"Yeah."

I scanned the page, pretending to try and figure it out. There was an "erase extraneous data" option right in front of me, but clearly whatever was in here was valuable. Whatever I remembered, I could let Esp know.

"Is there a problem?"

"No," I said, hoping there was something to be found in what I'd managed to look at. "Just making sure this will actually do it."

I hit the button. The screen wiped clear. "Extraneous Information Clear. There we go." I was trying to remember what I'd seen—what was the Eon Drive?—when he surprised me with a hug.

This was the second time we'd been physically close, but the first time he'd done it on purpose. This time he smelled less like home and more like sweat. My heart still raced.

"I—"

And then it was over. He was grinning at me, that *stupid* smile, and we were still standing close. I hugged him back.

"*Thank you*," said Alexander, clearly relieved. "It wouldn't have been the end of the world—I mean, I don't think—but you have no idea how much of a relief that is."

"No problem," I said, a little breathless. He didn't really step away. Or let go.

"Come with me," Alexander said.

"I can't."

"You want to."

"I *really* can't. The Prism Witches will take the blame if I vanish. It could start a war. And I've got a job to do here."

Alexander let me go. He didn't step away, but for once I couldn't read him. Which was odd. So far he'd been easy to read. "I guess I'll see you around, then."

"Yeah."

We stood there for a moment. Alexander was the one who broke the silence. "I shouldn't trust you."

"I shouldn't *like* you," I said. "But... we are friends, aren't we? It's not just me. We connect."

"It's not just you," he said. "I *don't* trust you. But yeah. We connect."

I sighed. "I know. *Why?*"

"Beats me." His hand slipped into mine and squeezed. "I'll see you around, Letter Mage."

And then—lightly, quickly, on a whim—he kissed me.

I'd never been kissed before. It was different than a hug, or any of the other times I'd been close to another person: falling asleep on Annie's shoulder, hugging my moms, clasping someone's hand, those were all *grounding*. They made me feel safe. At home. Comfortable. When Alexander kissed me, however brief, I felt a rush of adrenaline. I felt like I could fly.

And without even trying, I summoned the Light.

The scrolls flared. The terminal flared. Light filled the room, bleaching it of any color—of any shades of gray—and engulfed us, blinded us, suspended us in the moment. It was different somehow. Before I'd only summoned small flashes, sparks, but this spark caught on fire. It blossomed. It *grew*.

When it faded we were standing apart. Alexander looked afraid. "That was *extremely* romantic," he said. "But we have to go. *Now.*"

"What? I told you, I'm—"

"Listen," he said. "There's a reason their security is so lax. When the Light is on, they can see *everything that happens*. They gather information from it. Everything from your actions to your heart rate. They already know I'm here. Last time they let me leave —let you leave—just to see what we'd do. Same as with the malware on the ship."

"But we used it to get in—"

"*Isolated*, not a part of their network—this is different."

"Then get *out* of here." I pushed him away. "I'll stall them, you can get off the moon."

"And what's going to happen to you, then, Aleph?" He wasn't moving.

"I don't know." I had a plan in mind. Maybe I could get away with a lie. But if they knew as much as Alexander said, I didn't want to say it out loud. "I'll figure something out. Go. Leave. I'm fine, they can't hurt me for the same reason I can't leave, okay?"

"I don't—"

"You don't want to leave me. I know. Very noble. Shut up

and *go.*"

Alexander turned and ran. I took an instant to watch him vanish into the snow and the darkness. Then I closed the doors behind him, heart pounding, and walked slowly back to the terminal. I backed out of the menu and went to "Search" instead, and typed in "Glottal Moon".

I held out a hand and Summoned again, and a strong white gleam shimmered above my fingertips. I could *do* it. I could do this. They couldn't deny me what I'd come here for, and now I had something they didn't want me to have.

I had the Light.

Things were about to change.

The search screen displayed a wealth of information on my home moon just as I heard the lift. I scanned the snippets of information as fast as I could. Nothing particularly condemning. UNIVERSITY VILLAGE: MAP. MASTER OF LETTERS: WILDE. HIGH LINGUIST: INGRESS.

PERSON OF INTEREST: ALEPH WORF-SAPIR.

I didn't manage to open the document under my name before Maiman Williams exited the lift, raised her hands, and turned out the Light.

Making Your Own
Sigil Alphabet

Part One: Choosing Your Concentration

Everyone's personal magic system is different: paper, fire, and blood magic are only a few of the choices. A Letter Mage can do anything they want, provided they can narrow it down to 5 basic concepts.

A sigil alphabet is made up of 25 letters: 20 consonants and 5 vowels. Vowels are used to represent the major concepts of your magic system, and consonants are used to manipulate those concepts. If you *really* need more core concepts, W and Y can be recruited as vowels as well.

As an example, here is Dr. Kenning's chosen concepts for blood magic:

A: Blood	B: Clean	L: Avoid	T: Linger
E: Bone	D: Clot	M: Barrier	V: Contain
I: Body	F: Attach	N: Flow	X: Spread
O: Breath	G: Separate	P: Rhythm	Z: Consciousness
U: Bacteria	H: Increase	Q: Disrupt	
W: Temperature	J: Decrease	R: Sensation	
Y: Water	K: Here	S: Dissolve	

In Aleph's writing system, they don't use the letter C: the letters K and S stand in instead.

To make your own sigil alphabet, write out the 5 vowels and 20 consonants. Then sit and think about what magic system you want to create. Narrow it down to five major concepts, and apply them to A, E, I, O, and U.

Once you have those down, let your imagination run wild: how can you manipulate those concepts? What do you want to do with them? Assign those ideas to your consonants. Remember: try to keep your consonants as universal and flexible as possible. They can stack on each other to create specific effects.

In the next installment, we will cover the creation of your sigils.

Making Your Own
Sigil Alphabet

Part Two: Learn to Write the Foundation Alphabet

Sigil alphabets can be created from any writing system, but the tradition of the Glottal University is to use the Foundation Alphabet (transcribed crudely below).

The Foundation Alphabet is derived from a signaling system used in the Old University. Before the Colleges ascended to the moons, students used the symbols as a replacement text to pass coded messages between departments. The symbols are simple and quick to draw, and were easily passed off as notation or scribbles to prying eyes. During the days of coded messages, there were several different standards for grammar and writing direction, but modern Foundation is simply written left-to-write in lines, just like the text you're reading now.

The alphabet is reproduced below.

A	ᵌ	J	ᵍ	R	℗	Z	♭
B	ℬ	K	⅄	S	ℴ		
D	δ	L	τ	T	ℳ		
E	ℶ	M	μ	U	℘		
F	φ	N	ν	V	⅃		
G	⅄	O	ℳ	W	☯		
H	ℐ	P	℘	X	℥		
I	◠	Q	℧	Y	ℨ		

Making Your Own
Sigil Alphabet

Part Three: Create Your Sigils

Once the concepts and writing system are defined, a Letter Mage is ready to begin the process of creating sigils. We'll walk through this process using Dr. Kenning's concepts.

As a reminder, these are the concepts in Dr. Kenning's sigil alphabet:

A: Blood
E: Bone
I: Body
O: Breath

B: Clean
D: Clot
F: Attach
G: Separate

L: Avoid
M: Barrier
N: Flow
P: Rhythm

T: Linger
V: Contain
X: Spread
Z: Consciousness

U: Bacteria
W: Temperature
Y: Water

H: Increase
J: Decrease
K: Here

Q: Disrupt
R: Sensation
S: Dissolve

And here they are reproduced in Foundation text:

A: ♭ ⟨⟨⟨ ⟨⟨⟨ ♭
E: ♭ ⟨⟨⟨ ∨ ⟨
I: ♭ ⟨⟨⟨ ♭ ♪
O: ♭ ℘ ⟨ ♪ ⟨⟨ ♪
U: ♭ ♪ ⟨⟨ ⟨ ℘ ⟨⟨ ♪
W: ⟨⟨ ⟨ µ ⟨ ⟨ ℘ ♪ -
⟨⟨⟨⟨ ℘ ⟨
Y: ⟨⟨⟨ ♪ ⟨⟨ ⟨ ℘

B: ⟨ ⟨ ⟨ ♪ ∨
D: ⟨ ⟨ ⟨⟨ ⟨⟨
F: ♪ ⟨⟨ ♪ c ♪
G: σ ⟨ ⟨ ♪ ℘ ♪ ⟨⟨ ⟨

H: ⟨⟨ ∨ ⟨ ℘ ⟨ ♪ σ ⟨
J: ♭ ⟨ ⟨ ℘ ⟨ ♪ σ ⟨
K: ⟨ ⟨ ℘ ⟨
L: ♪ ⟨ ⟨⟨ ⟨⟨ ♭
M: ♭ ♪ ℘ ℘ ⟨⟨ ⟨ ℘
N: φ ⟨ ⟨⟨ ⟨⟨⟨
P: ℘ ⟨ ⟨ ⟨⟨ ⟨⟨ µ
Q: ♭ ⟨⟨ σ ℘ ⟨⟨ ⟨ ⟨⟨
R: σ ⟨ ∨ σ ♪ ⟨⟨ ⟨⟨ -
⟨⟨ ∨
S: ♭ ⟨⟨ σ σ ⟨⟨ ⟨ ♭ ⟨
T: ⟨ ⟨⟨ ∨ ⟨ ⟨ ℘
V: ⟨ ⟨⟨ ∨ ⟨⟨ ♪ ⟨⟨ ∨

X: σ ⟨ ℘ ⟨ ♪ ♭
Z: ⟨ ⟨⟨ ∨ σ c⟨⟨ -
⟨⟨ ⟨⟨ σ ∨ ⟨ σ σ

For translation assistance, refer to the table above.

The creation of a sigil is half precision and half artistic vision: all letters of the concept must be included in the sigil, but they do not need to be in any order or particular shape. This allows for creativity, but also requires careful thought. In the High College of the Glottal Moon, aspiring Letter Mages take classes in arrangement and design. Some elect to study anagrams, palindromes, poetry—which are all capable of producing powerful effects.

Today, however, we are focusing on the basics.

For our example, we'll use the first concept: the letter A, which is connected to "blood". First, the mage gathers the letters...

Second, the mage arranges the letters in several ways until they find something they enjoy: see the next page for arrangements.

Finally, the mage cleans the sigil into a final image to be used in practice. Once a sigil is created, it can be combined with other letters of its unique alphabet to cast spells.

Remember: the releasing of a sigil can be dangerous. Keep safety in mind when casting spells.

The Letter Mage: First Quarto

A spell is cast by "releasing" the image into the world, which is accomplished by destroying the sigil in whatever medium it has been created in. This can be accomplished by burning spell-inked paper, but also in more creative ways: a sigil burned on skin healing slowly over time, a sigil formed in colored sand dissolving from wind and entropy, or even just a carving in ice melting over time.

Remember: a Letter Mage must be responsible when casting magic. Once a spell is released, it can't be taken back.

THE SEA IN
THE SKY
-interlude-

Alexander loved the sky.

Back home, the stars were clear enough to kiss the sea, and the sea was clear enough to breathe in the stars. On nights when he didn't have to work, or didn't have a project, or didn't have a thousand other things to do, Alexander would sneak down to the beach and drift on the water. He'd imagine he was floating in celestial space. That was back before he'd ever broken atmo. He'd had no idea what floating in space felt like.

Now, in transit between moons, he could drift for real. And he'd been right.

There was nothing quite like looking out the window and seeing the expanse of your home planet slowly sinking away, or watching the stars shine like fairy dust, or observing the lazy dance of the seven satellites. It was enough to make a man feel at home.

Almost.

Alexander kept an eye on his descent. The great emerald jungle below was complicating things.

About
THE LETTER MAGE

- - -

The Letter Mage is an experiment.

Serial literature has been falling out of fashion since the early 1900s, but I went ahead and got into the genre anyways. Blame my mother for raising me on *Sherlock Holmes*: it made me very passionate about an extremely impractical idea. As a serialized story, *The Letter Mage* is unpublishable by most mainstream venues. Traditional publishing isn't set up for serial fiction (how would it fit into the model?) and most journals and magazines won't even consider work that comes in more than three parts. It thrives in the free online market, but unfortunately flourishing in a wonderful community doesn't usually pay the bills.

However, *The Letter Mage* wouldn't fit itself into any other form. In 2016, I attempted to write this story as a NaNoWriMo novel and failed miserably. Aleph's story was long and episodic, and as a straightforward novel would clock in at roughly 150-200,000 words. Not the longest novel in the world, but wandering and character-driven in a way that hasn't been in vogue since the early twentieth century. So in March of 2017, I sat down and wrote the first three installments, plotted out the rest of the story, gathered up a team of beta readers, and opened up a Patreon account.

The Letter Mage has *thrived* there.

Don't let anyone tell you serial literature is dead.

Installments are published every 1-2 months, and interludes at every $10 donation milestone. Patrons get early access to the stories as well as special rewards like shoutouts on the dedication page, paintings of sigils from the stories, and even customized sigils of their names. Quartos like this one are released for those who prefer a more traditional format, and often include unreleased extras.

About The Author
ALEXANDRA PENN

Alexandra Penn grew up in the museum wilds of Washington, DC. She learned the first thirteen letters of the alphabet before she got sentences down, watched the final shuttle launch from the fire escape outside Launch Control, and has been a certified Scuba diver since age twelve. She likes dogs, long walks on the beach, and defending the proletariat. Also books.

Alexandra is the Director of Iowa nonprofit The Writers' Rooms, an editor for hire, an amateur linguist and conlanger, and a Taurus. Her work has received several accolades, including an honorable mention in the 2017 Writer's Digest Annual Writing Contest. She spends all her free time on Twitter.

Support The Author

PATREON
WWW.TheLetterMage.com

WEBSITE
AlexandraPenn.squarespace.com

TWITTER
@AlexPenname

FACEBOOK
@AlexPenname

CPSIA information can be obtained
at www.ICGtesting.com
Printed in the USA
FSOW01n2006291017
40479FS